Days of Daisies

The Oaktown Series

Attic.doc and *Days of Daisies* celebrate their characters' sexy queer lives over the course of one year in their beloved Oakland, California—with jaunts to Berkeley, San Francisco, and Portland—while also diving deep into themes of death, identity, and belonging.

See oaktown.dagmarmiura.com.

Days of Daisies

Teja Rhae Watson

DAGMAR MIURA
LOS ANGELES

Published by Dagmar Miura
Los Angeles
www.dagmarmiura.com

Days of Daisies

First published 2025

ISBN: 979-8-89195-064-1

for Ocean, my Phoenix

Wasn't it death that taught me
to stop measuring my lifespan by length,
but by width? Do you know how many beautiful things
can be seen in a single second? How you can blow up
a second like a balloon and fit infinity inside of it?

—Andrea Gibson

Part 1:
Oakland

Chapter 1

When the cute skateboarder in her writing class asked her out for ice cream at the end of class, Anna could only nod. She followed Sam and her skateboard, tucked behind her backpack, down the hall and out into the sun.

As they walked down the front steps of Berkeley City College, Anna put on her sunglasses, then pulled off her cardigan and stuffed it in her bag. She was wearing a yellow and blue plaid sundress and considered a covert dab of red lip gloss but felt too self-conscious, in front of this perfectly unadorned butch. She doubted Sam had ever been self-conscious in her life.

Sam looked over at Anna, checking her out as they walked. Anna had *no idea* what Sam saw but at least she was wearing her fluffy honey-colored hair down, to provide some cover.

"You cool with the $1 place?" Sam asked. She had on tight black jeans and a loose T-shirt that said The Vandals, with a heart cracked open by a lightning bolt. Taller than Anna, with dark hair and eyes, and a solidity, a sureness that felt safe somehow.

Anna nodded again, relieved that Sam hadn't suggested one of the chichi places that always had lines down the block. She could never understand how people were willing to wait in line for ice cream. Who were these people?

Did they not have jobs, kids, bills?

They arrived at the ice cream parlor, its only customers. Anna pointed to butter brickle when Sam asked what she wanted, and Sam ordered rocky road. Sam paid the two bucks and they went back out onto Shattuck Avenue.

"You wanna walk a little?" Sam asked, and Anna nodded.

She didn't know what to say to someone like Sam; watching from her seat in the back of class, Anna had been fascinated by how effortlessly cool she seemed. It had been years since she'd been on a date—not that this was a date!—and she really didn't know how people did it without having a panic attack.

Her own contributions to their class discussions—had any of it had been even remotely intelligent? She couldn't remember.

Just eat your ice cream, she told herself.

The busyness of downtown Berkeley was a good distraction. Usually it irritated her, when she was running errands, hustling to class, trying to make a BART train. She was *always* rushing, she realized. She couldn't remember the last time she had just strolled with an ice cream cone. If Phoenix were here she'd be catching his drips, making sure his scoop didn't fall to the ground, avoiding nefarious men in their path. There was one guy she always saw down here who would walk straight toward you, fast, as if he wanted to run you over. If you moved, he moved the same way, blocking you, until at the last minute he swerved out of the way. It was unsettling, though Phoenix always laughed, like it was a game.

It was like she'd stepped out of class and into another version of her life. She stepped into the street to cross Shattuck and Sam put her arm out to stop her just as a bus whooshed past them, the driver shooting Anna a dirty look. Anna just stared at him, dazed, her hair flying wild around her in the bus's wake.

"Okay, now we can go," Sam said, and put her arm on Anna's back for just a moment. Anna felt a tingle spread through her body from this second of contact, and a smile of surprise spread across her face. No one had ever made her feel so much from so little.

Anna looked back at Sam, wanting her to explain it somehow. But Sam was focused on navigating them through the crowd of pedestrians.

At the commercial strip in the middle of Shattuck, Sam asked, "Do you wanna just sit here?" A wet marshmallow was slipping down her hand and she caught it with her mouth.

Anna nodded yet again and they sat on the curb right in the middle of the busy street, cars whizzing by inches from their feet. Anna saw that a brown trail of Sam's ice cream was headed for a long scrape on her forearm. With her free hand, she took the napkin she'd stuffed in her pocket and wiped the ice cream off Sam's wrist.

She felt her face flame as Sam stared at her. "Sorry," Anna said, her first word to Sam an apology, and as soon as it was out she wanted it back. She wanted to craft and shape her words like they did in writing class, but there was no time, it was happening *now.*

Sam just grinned at her and said, "I don't mind. It's been a while since someone cleaned up my mess." Her smile was lopsided, and her eyes were bright; she wasn't wearing sunglasses, and Anna could see right into their brown depth, like a tunnel to the inside of her. Anna felt like she was being sucked in.

She pulled her eyes away. There was a homeless guy ranting behind them; a fast-walking college kid gave them a dirty look as they passed, for taking up precious pedestrian space. The skull on Sam's shoulder grinned at Anna and Sam licked her ice cream nonchalantly, as if she sat in the middle of the street eating ice cream every day. It felt like how Anna had always imagined New York City would feel. She felt alive. For the first time in how long?

The big things of her life—the job, the kid, the bills—had taken over everything, like a virus.

"So why are you taking a writing class?" Sam asked.

No one had ever asked her that, and she wasn't sure how to explain it. It felt important to get it right. She said, "I need to make something. I don't know what it is yet. Something that's mine."

Sam said, "Me too. I mean, I'm starting a blog, I think I mentioned in class, and it's gonna be about skating, because do you know there are zero blogs by women skaters? But you know, 'women skaters,' I don't really connect with that either. I am kind of half-girl, half-boy, and I want to write about that too. I want it to be for everyone who doesn't feel like…themselves."

Anna could tell Sam wanted to say more, and Anna wanted to know more. But they licked their ice cream instead, watching each other. Sam put her tongue out flat and turned the cone around and around, catching all the drips. Anna put her whole mouth around the top of her cone and sucked on it, and smiled.

As Sam walked Anna to her car, she said, "You mentioned in class the other day that you have a kid. How old?"

"He's five. He's starting kindergarten soon. At the school where I teach, actually. I teach first grade, at Peralta." That broke the spell a little. Back to the old life.

"That'll be sweet for him, I bet, having you there."

She smiled at Sam wistfully. "This has been nice, to get to be the kid for a minute."

"It was nice for me too," Sam said. "Would you like to hang out again? We could go bowling. You could bring him if you want."

"Do I have to?" Anna said, and they laughed. The laugh unbuckled something that had been laced up tight in her. "Friday he's sleeping over with his friend." This wasn't technically true, yet, but it could be. She would ask Clara and Clara would say yes.

"Friday works for me," Sam said. "That's just two days from now."

A swarm of butterflies stormed Anna's belly.

Sam reached into her back pocket, then took Anna's hand, and placed her card face-up in her palm. SAM STRAY, it said in a simple font, and underneath, TATTOOS. "Text me your address," Sam said, "and I'll come pick you up. At seven?"

Anna nodded yet again, looking shyly away, and her eyes fell on Sam's chest, which looked totally flat. She saw that through the heart and the lightning bolt, "last chance for romance" was written in cursive. *It's a sign.*

"This is me," Anna said, nodding at her white Prius, parked on a small side street near school.

"Sweet ride," Sam said, and Anna let out another big laugh.

"Thanks for the ice cream," Anna said as she got in the car. Sam gently pushed her door closed and said "I'll see you soon," thumping twice on the roof of the car.

She started walking away down the middle of the street, looked back at Anna through the windshield with a satisfied grin, then pulled her skateboard out and in one movement tossed it down, stepped on, and pushed off with her left foot.

Push, push, and away.

Anna watched her go, silhouetted against the yellowing sky, composing the text she would send, the outfit she would wear.

PHOENIX

Hi. My name's Phoenix. My mama says it's because when I was born I flew out of her! Phoenixes have lots of colors on their tail, like a rainbow.

Phoenix is hard to spell but it's P-H-O-E-N-I-X. It has an X in it, which is lots of points in Scrabble. My name makes fifty-four points if you put it on the double-word score, with the X on the double-letter place, which I always start the game like that. Mama says that's not how other people play but we do because it's called a handicap for me because Mama knows lots more words than I do yet.

My mama is Anna. She's—Mama, how old are you?—she says thirty-six. Wow. That sounds like too many. Mama is shaking her head at me. What, Mama? She's writing down everything I say.

Mama started writing lately for a class she's taking so I wanted to write too. She says she has been waiting for her whole life to start writing so it's good I'm starting now while I'm a kid. I am only five so Mama is typing for me.

Mama and I live in Oakland. I was born in Oakland, actually I was born in this house we live in, not in a hospital because Mama doesn't like them. Whenever someone asks me where I live I say, "I live in Oaktown, G!" The person always laughs but the laugh always sounds different. I like to see what the laugh will sound like when I meet a new person.

Mama and I have a garden behind our house and we love to play there. But I wanted to tell you about the daisies. You that I'm writing to are my dad that I never met. Maybe we can send you my story when I finish it.

Mama and I went on an adventure this month. She called it a road trip. She said it very excited when we left, like "Road trip!!!" We drove all day. I didn't really like that part. I had books though and even a special machine that plays movies. I watched *My Neighbor Totoro*. Have you seen it? If not, you would really like it.

Anyway after we drove all day with only stopping to pee, we saw a place like a mountain. Mama says it's called a dune. A mountain made of sand. I never knowed there was something like that! It was really fun to roll down. I did it lots of times. I still have sand in my hair. Actually that was why Mama wouldn't roll down with me, she didn't want to get sand in her hair. That was her being boring.

After I rolled to the bottom, I heard big noises like monsters. Mama said they were motorcycles on the other side of the hill. It was weird to hear them but not see them. Mama didn't like that they were there and she got a cloud in her face, but just for a second because we were having too much fun to be cloudy. We also walked through a funny little forest, like in *Totoro*, and then out of the trees and more sand, and then another forest, with cool flowers. Then we walked up, up, up another sand hill, dune, and then when we came to the top we looked over the edge and there was the ocean.

Of course I know the ocean already because we go there all the time, but I didn't know it was there where we were too and I was soooooooooooooo happy to see it. Mama yelled "Surprise!!!" and then we ran so fast down the hill and into the water. Mama didn't even care that my shoes and clothes got wet, and hers too. She swung me up in the air and then swooped me along the water like a seagull.

One time this person who I don't like told me a phoenix was not a real bird and I got so mad. He might be at my new school. I am going to big-kid school next month, called Peralta Elementary. It's where Mama works. She teaches the first graders and I will be in the first grade, which is kindergarten. Wait, but why is it called kindergarten and not first grade if it is the first grade? Mama says she doesn't know. Life doesn't make sense sometimes.

I am not very happy about going to kindergarten because I love my school where I go now. Even though the stupid boy goes there. His name is George—such a stupid name—and I really hope he does not go to Peralta. I am like crossing my fingers that doesn't happen.

Me and Mama are pacifists, which means when George pushes me down I just have to ignore him. I give him a look, a *glare,* that means he is bad and stupid and I really want to say it out loud too but I know he knows what I am thinking.

Mama says at home I can say whatever I want because it doesn't hurt her like it would hurt George. She says that's how grown-ups do it, they bite their tongues all the time. She says it doesn't hurt your actual tongue but it does hurt inside of your body and that's why it's good to let it out sometimes, like in a scream or any noise really.

Aaaaaaaaaaaaaaaaaaaaaaaaaargh!

We have to be a little quiet because of our old neighbor Susie but Mama's right, I do feel a little better.

Bye for now!

Chapter 2

*W*hen Anna opened her front door, she could see hope in Sam's eyes. She was wearing a black T-shirt, black jeans, and teal Adidas, and she was carrying a helmet.

Anna invited her in, the butterflies returning, a tumult of color darting around inside her. She had chosen a red and white vintage dress and gold platforms, and her yellow hair was loose, with her usual red lipstick. It felt like too much now.

But Sam, whose hair was pushed up into a pompadour, said, "Cute outfit," and Anna relaxed.

She showed Sam around the apartment, half of a duplex that she had lived in since before Phoenix was born. Sam complimented Phoenix's drawing of a phoenix, framed above the couch. "I just did a phoenix tattoo last week. I like his better."

Anna grabbed her jean jacket, and they left on Sam's black Vespa. Anna felt terribly self-conscious, at first, even in her helmet, out in the open—like she was on display. She commonly ran into her students and their parents out in the world and for this one night she wanted to be anonymous, kid-free.

Soon she forgot to care. Sam didn't go too fast—the scooter couldn't go very fast—though a couple times Anna gasped at a car swerving a little too close to comfort. But then they were fine and she laughed a little hysterically and held Sam tighter. Their bodies already felt comfortable together, but how was that possible?

Don't think too much, she told herself.

They took San Pablo Avenue to the Albany Bowl. Anna hadn't liked this bowling alley much when she'd been there with kids, but on this night it was good. Quiet, not too much testosterone. They each had a beer, then they shared one, and then they shared another.

They bowled two games and Anna won both. Sam said, "I've had my ass kicked at bowling a few times before, but never quite like that."

Their attraction was like another entity between them. Anna had never felt anything like it. With guys, the attraction was implied, because of what both knew was coming at the end of the night. This time, she didn't know what was to come, having never been with a woman before. But whatever it was, she wanted it.

They touched more as the night went on, bumping into each other "accidentally" on their way to and from the lane. "Oops, so sorry," they said. "Excuse me, pardon me." Bowling was perfect because it kept them busy and moving. Anna couldn't have sat down—forget seeing a movie or having dinner—with the electricity between them buzzing her into a frenzy. The only way to release it was to move.

When they did sit, to eat the string beans with tofu and fried rice they'd ordered from the attached Chinese place, they sat right next to each other. Sam leaned over and kissed Anna's neck—just a peck, but it sent a shock through Anna's body, and she actually jumped out of her seat, without meaning to.

"Maybe we should go to your place," Anna said then,

and she could tell Sam was relieved that it was being turned on, not off, that had caused Anna to jump away from her.

But Sam said, "Not yet," and smiled. "Let's play one more game."

"You're just dying to beat me, aren't you?"

"I really am," Sam said.

But she didn't. Anna said, "Do I get to decide what we do next, since I won?" When Sam nodded, Anna said, "Let's go to your place."

They changed back into their shoes, Anna's platforms making her almost as tall as Sam, and they left the bowling alley, eyeing each other from this new perspective.

The ride to Sam's was exquisite: Anna's arms around Sam's waist, Sam's capable body up against hers but Anna the one holding her. It gave her a sense of control that she needed. As they wove up, up, up through the El Cerrito hills, she looked behind her and saw the bay, and San Francisco glittering behind it. Her insecurities faded into the horizon.

Anna's sandal tangled in the Vespa's footrest as she tried to dismount, and she stumbled, tried to catch her balance, and toppled into the grass. Suddenly Sam was on her knees, straddling her. The stars were all lit up like fairies rooting for them, and Sam's face so serious above her, her very own moon.

It wasn't just some butch act, and Anna knew because Sam stared at her, then said, "You're real, alright."

Anna could see in her eyes that Sam was scared of what she felt, of the power Anna already had over her. She laced her fingers through Anna's and plunged their hands into the grass above Anna's head, and then she kissed her.

It was the softest.

Thing.

Anna had ever felt.

She opened her eyes and watched Sam, the line of her jaw, her eyes closed; she looked to Anna like a teenage boy, and the newness of this was thrilling. Anna closed her eyes and felt herself melt.

And then suddenly Sam pulled her up, threw her over her shoulder, and carried her into the house, Anna's dress riding high. Inside, Sam pulled her shoes off and tossed Anna gently onto the couch.

Sam made a fire, then, while Anna watched her, her movements spare and intelligent, her shoulders straining against her T-shirt, her neck with the heart tattooed on the back. Her place was simple and clean, stylish. A big white shag rug lay in front of the fire, and when Sam turned around Anna was lying on it, her lips still stained red, a piece of grass stuck in her hair. She'd left her dress behind on the couch.

Sam looked down at her like her heart was breaking.

She took off her pants, her eyes not leaving Anna's, and joined her on the rug in her black T-shirt and slim black boxers. They propped themselves up on their elbows, looked into each other's eyes. What Anna saw was an infinity of depth, enough to explore forever.

Whatever Sam saw in Anna's eyes made her eyes fill with tears—just to the brim. Her eyes changed from brown to green and that was all the encouragement Anna needed.

She climbed up on top of Sam, and they started. They were starting something together, she could feel it. Whatever they were doing, it was serious, and she knew it was mutual.

And it felt like they did it all. Anna realized, as it was

happening, that she had dreamed of it, had imagined what it might feel like with a woman, and it was a million times better than she ever could have imagined. She laughed and screamed and cried. Sam owned her own little bungalow, at the end of a street with no neighbors, so Anna let herself be loud. Anna wanted Sam to break her open and she did. She wanted Sam to make her forget it all and she did. Anna wasn't a mama anymore, wasn't a teacher, wasn't a woman or a daughter or a sister.

She was a lover. She was made for this. How could she not have known, how much she had been made for this?

They kissed for hours. They held each other so tight their arms got sore. They learned each other's bodies. Anna kissed all of Sam's tattoos and introduced herself. "Nice to meet you, seahorse. You too, willow tree. Hey, tiger—I'm Anna."

They took a bath. They drank a bottle of champagne. They had more sex. Sam deflowered Anna thoroughly and effectively. They talked about what they didn't like. They ordered a pizza in the middle of the night. Sam ran outside naked and Anna followed, and they fucked in the wind, Sam's hand inside Anna, almost all the way up inside....

Anna Harvey
Creative Writing Assignment #2. Describe (but don't name) something memorable. Instead of telling what it was, tell how it felt in your body. (150 words)

My toes are pinched again and I float a little higher. One leg swings around, my knees bend. Muscles contract and release in tandem with another's but my hands clasp on to each other.

I feel a breeze tickling my neck and a pressure against my hips. My body is vibrating like a tuning fork.

But then the ears go empty and the buzzing in my limbs stops. My hands let go of each other. Feet go to meet earth, and miss.

The softness is restorative, a primal need satisfied. A swelling in my heart comes and goes, ebbs and flows, then builds to a tsunami in my stomach, a void in my head.

Every part of me is coming to life. Parts I didn't even know I had, awakening. Like I was buried treasure… everything in me held up to the light after way too long in the dark.

PHOENIX

The other day what I wanted to write about was the DAISIES!!! I remembered when I was going to sleep and I wanted to write them then but Mama said the computer was closed and I should dream about them instead.

This is for my dad, so that if he ever meets me he can read this and know about me. Mama says she doesn't think that will happen but she says you never know. Life is a mystery. That means you never know what's hiding around the corner. If it was my dad hiding around the corner I would be happy.

So, the daisies were maybe the most best thing I have ever seen in my WHOLE life. What happened was we were driving home from our camping trip. Mama did something funny because she's worried if she only uses machines she will forget how to use her brain. So she turned off our map lady in our car, which we call Sheila. She wanted to get home without Sheila telling her what to do. But then, because of that we got kind of lost. *(Note from Mama: We were not lost.)*

Well, Mama says we weren't lost, but we were definitely not going the right way, because Mama was worried even though she pretended not and REFUSED to turn Sheila back on to help us. She even bought a map from a store guy and asked him where we were but he didn't know.

When I think of it now, it feels like a dream. And like a mystery. We didn't know what would be around the corner and we liked that. We were on an adventure to find something new. And do you know what we found?

DAISIES!!! An enormous, giant field of them. All

daisies everywhere for as far as I could see, millions of daisies, which are Mama's favorite flower! It was like all the daisies in the world, a giant family of them. They looked like a big huge cloud with a million yellow eyes looking at us.

We got out of the car and went into them gently. They were up around my belly, and they tickled me. It was like we were swimming in them. And we got to the middle of them and lay down on a bed of them, on our backs. We looked up at the sky and the daisies WERE all one big cloud holding us like a hug.

When I looked around, they were dancing in the wind, all around us so many designs. It was their world and we went into it, we wanted to be with them more than in the car, or anywhere. It was the most special place I ever saw.

I wanted to sleep in the daisies but Mama said it wasn't good for them and anyway wouldn't we be happier in our own beds?

And guess what? After we got back in the car Mama STILL refused to ask Sheila for help, but this time she found our way back to the big road and Mama said the reason for us getting lost was for the daisies! So we could find them.

I can still see them when I close my eyes.

Mama says that's a good place to stop because it's bedtime. Good night!

Anna Harvey

Creative Writing Assignment #3. Create a short story that is twenty-six sentences long, each sentence beginning with the next letter of the alphabet.

Angriness is ingrained in me. Because that's how she was. Cold, a chill that never thawed. Dad didn't believe me when I told him. "Every day she wakes up smiling," he said. Finally I showed the bruises from my mother hitting me against the wall. "Great," Dad said. "Happy now?" Invisibility ran in my family. Jettisoned the truth. Kept us in check. Leaving, it turned out, was not only the solution but also the cure.

My girlfriend would only want to punish if she knew, if she was my girlfriend. No way I'll tell her. Obviously it's for me to deal and no one else. Phoenix will never feel that... Quietude, quickening. Rage, it's not worth it. Silence is easier. Trusting no one. Understanding aloneness. Very quietly squelching it. What I feel is not worth believing. X it out. You think it really happened. Zilch is what happened.

Chapter 3

*A*nna read what she'd written the night before and couldn't believe how much anger she still felt. She didn't understand how feeling so great, this thing with Sam, could turn into feeling so bad.

That's what happens when you drink a whole bottle of champagne by yourself, she reminded herself. Teaching hungover had really sucked.

The night before, Anna had opened a bottle of champagne, thinking maybe Sam would come over after work, that they could reenact the other night.

She had spent the entire weekend after their first date unable to think about anything but Sam. Wondering if what she thought had happened could possible have really happened.

In class yesterday they had both been super self-conscious; they sat next to each other but didn't really talk and didn't touch at all except for a quick hug. After class Sam had a tattoo she had to get back to at the shop. Anna thought about asking if she could come with her, since she had two hours to kill before picking up Phoenix, but it seemed too desperate.

Instead she ordered a lemon drop at the hotel bar by City College. Then she picked up Phoenix and they went home and had dinner and then Anna, hoping she would see

Sam soon—she had said she would call when she was done with work—popped the champagne. It felt pretty good at first, when Anna was thinking Sam would come over, any minute; she would be tipsy and it would be endearing, and they would drink the last of the bottle together.

But by the last glass, Sam still hadn't called and Anna just felt pathetic. Then Anna wrote that terrible ABC assignment. Finally she passed out, and *then* Sam called. She left a message saying she had worked till midnight, tattooing a big back piece.

Anna felt like she should be happy, so why did she feel angry? Tonight she had snapped at Phoenix for asking for another cookie when she'd already told him no. The look on his face was awful, like he was scared of her. She knew that feeling well.

You said you'd never be like her, she reminded herself.

Anna hadn't thought about her mother in so long. The fucking champagne had brought it all back: her mom's drink of choice.

And now, since she and Sam were sharing their assignments with each other before they turned them in, giving feedback, either Anna would need to write a new ABC story or she'd have to show Sam the drunken one.

She'd never told anyone about the abuse. She just never wanted to talk about it; talking about it would have made it feel real. Instead Anna just made sure that her mother was the only one who would ever hurt her like that.

After leaving home at the earliest opportunity, Anna could see red flags from a mile away and just completely detoured around those people. Finally she gave up on even trying to be in a relationship.

She didn't know how to tell Sam this—not only had she never been with a woman, she hadn't really ever been in a relationship. The short-term things were just flings. She never let them in. It was easier that way.

And after Phoenix was born, the logistics of being with someone just became too difficult. And anyway she hadn't been attracted to anyone for years, before Sam.

But Anna was afraid to tell Sam this. Already there was the kid thing. Anna wouldn't blame her if it was too much to take on; she wouldn't want to be a parent to someone else's kid. But she couldn't hide Phoenix, obviously. Sam seemed to like him, anyway.

And she knew Sam liked her. She thought Sam might even be falling for her.

She was clearly falling for Sam, and it made her want to run like hell, away from here, from her. Now that she'd finally found what she'd been looking for her whole life without even knowing it…she couldn't deal with losing it.

I can't lose my shit again, Anna thought. She couldn't put Phoenix through that again, she couldn't risk losing her job.

Anna had finally gotten to a good place, where she felt strong, and now this thing with Sam was making her feel like a mess again. Seeing her life from Sam's point of view, it was all suspect. Her decision to have a baby on her own, her job that was not what she really wanted to be doing, her friends that she didn't really like, her family that was not in the picture, her house that was dirty, her neighborhood that she couldn't even walk around in at night—when she looked at it from Sam's perspective she saw a big fucking mess.

Sam was forty, she owned a house, she had a job she loved, good friends, and several relationships under her belt. A mom she was close to, who supported her. What must that be like? How could Anna compete?

What Anna had was Phoenix. He was her everything, because everything else had been on the back burner as she raised him. She had chosen this life. But suddenly it didn't seem like enough.

Sam was someone who followed through on every dream she ever had. When she'd wanted a skateboard at thirteen but her mom said no, she got a job and saved up the money and then bought her first board. She watched videos at the skate shop and made friends with the skaters there and did what they told her to do. She fought her fears and she got really good at skating.

They had made plans to hang out tomorrow. Claire couldn't watch Phoenix because her husband was home for once and the three of them were going to spend time together like a happy little family. Things had been awkward between Claire and Anna since Sunday. When Claire and Skyla were over, Anna started telling Claire about her awesome sex with Sam—to which Claire had held up a hand, like it was TMI. Anna couldn't believe it. She was probably jealous because she and Tim only had sex like once every other year.

Either way, Anna had to hire a babysitter. Which meant that she and Sam would only have a few hours to hang out. She was starting to feel like it wasn't even worth it. Phoenix was snoring loudly in his room, seemed like he might be getting sick. If he was worse tomorrow she wouldn't want to leave him with the sitter.

She started to text Sam to cancel, but a tiny voice deep inside her stopped her. *Wait*, it said. *Just wait until tomorrow.*

PHOENIX

Guess what? Mama wanted me so much that she made me all by herself, at home. Like baking a cake. Baking a kid! Ha.

She says there was just one ingredient that she didn't have and my dad—which I hope is you reading this—gave her the last ingredient. But then he had to go back to India so he couldn't know me and that's sad.

Sometimes it's a little lonely with just me and Mama. So we go to the park a lot or my friend Skyla and her mama come over to play. I have lots of dress-up clothes and wings so we can be birds and insects too. We fly around the house and the yard and down the street when our mamas are smoking on the front porch.

Cigarettes are very, very bad for you and Mama says I should never ever have one because they are like a bad magic spell that is hard to get out of. She most of the time can do it but sometimes the cigarettes are stronger than her. With Skyla's mom, they drink mama juice and they laugh a lot and we all dance. Until our old neighbor tells us to turn the music down!

Chapter 4

For their second date, Sam said she wanted to surprise Anna, if that was okay with her, and of course Anna said yes. Sam asked if she could drive them in Anna's "sexy electric car" and of course Anna said yes.

They drove over the new Bay Bridge, its white columns and palm trees inviting them in. Anna had been over it many times, but always while at the wheel, and she admired it from her passenger seat. She thought the bridge made San Francisco seem like a whole new city—more modern, more elegant.

When she started to feel guilty for leaving Phoenix with the babysitter, she counted in her head and realized this was only the fifth time in his life she had done that. The baby-sitter was the older sister of one of her students, and she was sweet and fun and Phoenix liked her. Anna reminded herself that he was safe and they were probably making chocolate chip cookies.

She let herself be driven. As downtown floated by to her right, she gazed at the buildings and the bay and thought, as she did every time, that it had to be the prettiest city in the whole world. She and Phoenix often talked of moving to SF, and would have if it weren't for her job. She loved her school, for herself and, soon, for Phoenix, so leaving Oakland wasn't really an option. She figured maybe they would move to SF for middle school and high school, but that felt like a lifetime away—in fact it *was* more than Phoenix's entire lifetime from now.

She looked over at Sam, at her boyish profile. Her face, viewed head-on, was soft and sweet, but everything else, how she presented herself to the world, was masculine. She looked like a skate punk—Anna couldn't believe it when she'd learned Sam was forty—with her scruffy hair, her tattoos, her boxers poking out of her jeans.

But those eyes, that was where she held her years. They had all the world in them. When Sam focused those eyes on Anna's, every single one of Anna's doubts and worries about what they were doing evaporated.

They exited and Sam cut through downtown. She was a confident driver, which let Anna relax and enjoy San Francisco passing her by. The downtrodden Tenderloin gave way to the expansiveness of Geary Street, until Sam pulled expertly into a parking spot in front of a Japanese market.

"Come with me," she said to Anna.

After picking up some snacks at the market—yakisoba noodles, sembe crackers, Pocky sticks, and cans of sweet coffee—they crossed the Japantown plaza. Anna had no idea where they were going. Sam was wearing black jeans and a black hoodie and she looked so cute, smiling in anticipation of the surprise. She wished Sam would hold her hand.

They came to a door—it looked like a temple, with a small fountain and a bell—and Sam pulled the door open for Anna and ushered her in, biting her bottom lip.

Inside, Sam asked, "Never been here?"

"No," Anna said.

"Oh, good," Sam replied, smiling big. "Two to soak," she said to the woman at the desk, who took Sam's credit card and then led them through an elegantly furnished hallway, explaining as she did that there were two pools—one hot, one cold—and two saunas—one dry, one wet. Sam thanked the woman and she left them in the dressing room.

Anna's eyes had gone wide with excitement. She gave Sam a big hug. "I haven't had a good soak in years," she said. "Thank you."

"You're welcome," Sam said.

Anna pulled off her sweater and shoved it in a locker. Sam's eyes lingered on Anna's black bra as she pulled off her hoodie and tossed it on top of Anna's sweater.

Inside the Kabuki bath area, Sam led Anna over to the Japanese-style shower stools. They washed themselves with the handheld nozzles, then walked over to the hot pool and climbed in. Sam explained that it was a women-only day, and they were there in full array: every shape, color, and age represented.

Instantly Anna's body relaxed. The water was very hot. She followed Sam over to the side of the pool, where they sat side by side. Anna put her head in her arms on the side of the pool and let her body float out behind her, closing her eyes and trying not to think about whether Sam was watching her ass, whether anyone was. Sam dunked her head and lay on her back for a while, eyes closed. With her hair wet her face looked more feminine, and even though she knew Sam didn't love her femininity, Anna had to admit that she did. The softness in her face. Those eyes.

Sam draped herself over the side of the pool, her face next to Anna's. And then Anna quietly said "I want you." It just came out, without her even thinking it first.

Sam nodded knowingly and, all business, scanned the place. Then she said quietly, "Watch where I go, and meet me there in a minute." She stood and gracefully pulled herself out of the water, drawing the stares of all the women in the pool. Even with the big tiger dominating her back, it was her ass that most of them were looking at. When they saw Anna watching them, they looked away.

Sam rounded a corner, to a part of the room that Anna couldn't see, and Anna felt a shiver go through her, despite the heat. She forced herself to close her eyes and count, and when she reached fifty she walked over to the steps and rose out of the pool, the nipples of her round breasts hard.

Around the corner, Anna saw a red curtain, and under the curtain she saw Sam's tattooed legs. She quickly pulled the curtain aside and stepped into the shower stall. In the corner, it felt protected, and too dark for anyone to see their two sets of feet.

Sam grinned and high-fived her. Anna fell into her and kissed her hard, her hands traveling all over her back and her butt, into her hair, pulling Sam toward her urgently. Anna had been waiting her whole life for this, and she couldn't wait any longer.

Sam took one of Anna's nipples into her mouth. She cupped Anna's mound and one finger snuck up and in, her thumb at Anna's clit. Anna moaned into Sam's hair, sucked her neck, her ear, the water beating on her face.

Sam had three fingers inside Anna now, and whispered, "I want to suck you but we better not press our luck." That would be too much to ask any Kabuki Hot

Springs employees who might see them to ignore; they did have a no-sex rule. So Sam sucked her other nipple instead, her hand pounding Anna from inside. Anna came quickly and quietly.

She draped her happy body over Sam's and sucked slowly on Sam's neck. She put her hand where it wanted to go, looked up for permission, and got a "Yes" in her ear from Sam. She started with her thumb, which slid wetly up and in. Anna thought she would pass out from how good it felt—the wetness that was all for her. She brought up more fingers and pressed them in, until almost her whole hand was inside. Anna had never liked her small hands but now she loved how it felt having her hand almost disappear inside her lover. Sam's eyes were closed, but her mouth was open, and it looked to Anna like Sam was feeling something she hadn't felt in a long time.

Sam pushed Anna up against the wall of the shower, and kissed her hard. Her small breasts rubbed against Anna's larger ones, and they both groaned. Sam rubbed herself up against their hands and she growled into Anna's ear, an animal cry. She panted into Anna's ear, catching her breath, and Anna thought she would cry. Being let in like that…

And then Sam slipped out of the shower, leaving Anna alone, eyes wide, mouth hanging open.

Anna found Sam in the wet sauna, with its white tile seats, and after hosing each other down they went together into the dry sauna, which was made of cedar. Anna loved both. She cuddled into Sam in the wood sauna and started to fall asleep. Sam startled her awake, whispering, "I gotta get out of here" and leaving the sauna. It felt healthy. She didn't want to be one of those couples who always had to do everything together.

When she left the dry sauna, she collided with a naked Sam coming out of the restroom area.

"There you are," Anna said with relief, smiling and falling against Sam. They hugged, right there in the doorway, for all the others to see, and Anna let everything she felt for Sam flow out of her and into Sam. She held her long and hard, and Sam held her back.

"You okay?" Sam asked in her ear, and Anna nodded. "You ready to go?" Anna nodded again, and they headed away from the baths. "Good. There's one more place I want to take you, if we have time."

"Okay. We have our treats too," Anna said as they walked to their locker.

"Oh, yeah!" Sam said, pulling out the plastic bag and popping open a can of sweet coffee, handing it to Anna, then taking a sip as Anna handed it back. "Mmm." She handed Anna a Pocky stick, and a bite of noodles, feeding her as she got dressed. Since it took Anna longer to get ready, it was a good system. By the time they gathered their things to go, Anna was awake and feeling good, her damp hair tied up and her lips stained red.

On their way out, in the hallway, Sam kissed her. Then she wiped her lips on the back of her hand and grinned like a teenager. They walked back out into a now-dark San Francisco, holding hands.

Back in the car, they floated down Geary. Anna let out a big, happy sigh. Funny, she thought, how sex could secure her head to her body, making her feel grounded and sure. What they were doing was special, something she'd never done before. Sam too seemed calmer, and Anna realized that there had been a nervous energy in her that was gone now. Maybe she'd been nervous about whether Anna would like her date idea.

"Thank you," she said. "That was perfect."

"I'm glad," Sam said, smiling sweetly at her. "It was good for me too."

They laughed.

Suddenly Geary ended, and Anna saw the ocean. Sam pulled into a little lot and parked. She leaned over and kissed Anna. Sam held Anna's head like she was something precious, like a nautilus shell she'd found on the ocean floor. Anna felt Sam's need for her even stronger than before.

They stopped kissing and looked out at the ocean. In the dark, Anna thought, it looked like it was full of secrets.

"I have to tell you, I really like you," Sam said, her eyes on the sea. "I haven't felt this way in a while."

"I like you too," Anna said quietly.

"You do?" Sam asked, looking over at Anna, her eyes bright.

"I do," Anna nodded.

"Good." Sam smiled and pulled the plastic bag from the backseat. She opened the yakisoba noodles and a pair of chopsticks, then slurped up some noodles.

As Sam ate, Anna looked back out at the water. She felt like Sam had just given her everything she needed to keep going with what they were doing, without worrying. She remembered how she'd felt just a few days ago, the champagne and the horrible attack of doubt.

Remember this, the next time that happens.

Anna loved that Sam didn't say too much. She didn't seem to need much from her, at least so far. She didn't need to know Anna's whole life story to know that she liked her. There was the way they felt together, which was stronger than anything Anna had ever felt with anyone, and that was enough for now.

She's an adult, Anna thought. *She knows what she wants. And right now that's me.*

So, as Sam drove them back over the Bay Bridge, and Anna realized she hadn't thought of Phoenix once all night, Anna resolved to let what was happening between Sam and her unfold naturally, and to stay out of its way.

PHOENIX

I am going to big-kid school in six days.

I am a little scared but Mama says I shouldn't be. She says I got the best teacher in the whole school. I will have Mama for my teacher next year, when I am in the first (really second) grade. If I am good. Mama says if I'm not good in kindergarten the lady who runs the school might put me in the other teacher's class, and I want that to not happen.

Mama says kindergarten will be fun. She said my teacher will read a book about a dragon. I do love dragons, though I can't say why. They are like phoenixes. Well, almost as cool.

I love talking to you! It's fun to think about what's in my head. Mama says there's a way for me to talk to the computer so it can write itself, without Mama having to do it. Then she could be making dinner while I talk to the computer what I want to write. That would be good for her, and also good for me because I love to eat!

In case you are wondering, some of my favorite foods are: noodles, pizza, sushi (without fish because I don't eat fishes), fruit especially peaches and blueberries, cereal especially the kind with the colored circles that Mama lets me have sometimes for a treat, and granola and raisins, I like to mix them together and pour the milk over, also of course pancakes and cookies that I can make almost all by myself. The hot part is scary so Mama does that.

What foods do you like? If you are my father reading this, I would especially like to know. I wonder if you like mangos. Mama says that in India you have mango trees on every street. I imagine you climbing up into a mango tree and eating mangos up there all day!

I also love mangos. Sometimes they taste like chocolate, which is weird, but I am not complaining because I LOVE chocolate. I wonder if there is a person who doesn't love chocolate. Mama is shaking her head no, she's never met one. Unfortunately we don't have so much chocolate anymore because it gives Mama headaches.

I think that's enough writing for today. I will tell you again soon about kindergarten. I am trying to be brave.

Transitions (Sam's blog) post 1:
Skating the Sea

Hey you guys!

Did you know there are no genderqueer skaters who blog? So here I am. Reprezent.

Skateboarding is this thing that compares to nothing else. Not sex, because sex is something you do with someone. Skating is all you. It's your own world that you create new each time.

Yeah, there's usually other people skating with you, but they're doing their own thing. The guy next to you is doing whatever he's doing, he's gonna stay out of your way, and if he can he'll watch your tricks, give you props if you landed it tight, or if you didn't but the effort was true. Skating is all about pushing yourself. We encourage each other.

The other skaters, they're not friends exactly, but I know them and they know me. I think they mostly see me as another guy, though some of them must be confused. The guys (yes, they are like 99% guys) at the Berkeley park have only seen me in my current more-male manifestation. Back when I skated Portola in S.F., I know lots of guys were definitely confused by me, as I morphed from female to male before their eyes. And the energy was more hardcore there, back then. I had to watch my back.

But mostly, the skate scene is cool. We're all doing the same crazy thing—diving headfirst into concrete. Over and over, again and again. Even after all the broken body parts and concussions we won't ever stop. We are a tribe in that way and I guess that comes before gender politics. They are the only place I've ever belonged.

Only other skaters know: the way you have to plan

ahead, the way you have to think fast, the way you have to pick yourself up and do it again, even when you're bleeding, until you nail it. You can't sleep at night until you do, you'll be lying in bed doing it over and over, obsessing, until you get it right—but oh man, when you do it's the best feeling on earth.

Lately I mostly just skate on my lunch break. The first part of my day, I'm anticipating the hills and valleys, they're pulling me to them like a magnet. By afternoon I'm edgy from the buzz of the tattoo gun and ready to get out. Most days I schedule long lunch breaks, but then sometimes I don't eat, because it's never enough time. I never want to stop skating. I always have to pull myself away. And then the rest of the day I'm remembering it in my bones. My body's still feeling it, the air especially, like the rocking of a boat in your body after you're on land again. When I fall asleep I'm thinking about whatever tricks I nailed that afternoon—that way maybe if I'm lucky I'll dream about skating. It does happen sometimes.

The jangle of the wheels, the quiet in the air, the crash back down. Waves cresting and crashing in my ears.

PHOENIX

Today I went swimming in a pool in the forest. We drove up, up, up until we could see San Francisco!

The best thing was the pool had salt in it! Like the ocean. Mama says the stuff they put in to make it clean was made of salt instead of the stinky stuff in normal pools. So it didn't hurt my eyes, and I swam all day! Skyla was with us and her mama too and at first it was just us because it was brrrr cold but then the sun came out and lots more people came. There were older kids and younger kids too and grown-ups and we all splashed around together. It was great! Skyla and I did lots of races. I am faster at swimming underwater and she is faster at above the water. I like to pretend I'm a fish or a sea serpent.

Finally we had to get out because the pool was closing and we went to the playground and played on the pirate ship. I fell down and got a splinter but I didn't cry. Mama says we have to take out the splinter after we do this writing, but I really don't think we should because it doesn't hurt much and the taking it out will hurt more.

Bye!

Chapter 5

*A*nna knew she had to tell Sam about her limited relationship experience, and she knew Sam was wondering who Phoenix's dad was. She figured she might as well get it over with. If Sam was spooked, it would be better if she left sooner rather than later.

One minimum day, on Sam's lunch break, they met at a park in Berkeley and lay on a blanket in the grass. They ate the gourmet snacks Anna had picked up, but even after drinking a bottle of the pear cider Sam had brought, Anna still felt awkward bringing it up. Finally, she told Sam she had something she wanted to tell her.

"I just, I wanted you to know, you know, I haven't been with any women before, as you know, but also I haven't really been in any relationships before either. You know, in my twenties, I had flings. They never lasted more than a month or two. I would get bored, or they would…they would want more, and I wouldn't. Maybe because they were guys, I'm realizing now."

Sam looked nonplussed by this info. Anna decided to keep going.

"Anyway, Phoenix's dad was a friend of a friend, named Rishi. We were never together, I just liked him a lot as a person. He was just such a good guy. He was here from India going to medical school. I knew that he wanted to be a parent, but not for a while—he wanted to get married, have a good job, a house, all that.

"I was having these hella strong maternal urges, and so one day I asked him if he would consider donating his sperm, so I could have a baby. I told him I would do it all on my own and never ask him for anything.

"He said yes. We had a special bond, maybe because we never slept together. We just had a very genuine affection for each other."

"Did he want to sleep with you, though?" Sam asked. "It sounds like maybe he did."

"I really don't think he did." Anna could see that Sam was getting jealous. Definitely not the reaction she'd been expecting. "We just weren't attracted to each other. It wasn't like that. He was kind of nerdy and short." Anna didn't think he was that much shorter than Sam, but she figured a little ego stroking wouldn't hurt.

Sam nodded, seemingly appeased, so Anna continued.

"We did some research and figured out the best way to inseminate at home. He would come into a warm bowl, in the other room, then bring it to me and help me insert it."

"What?! Insert what?!"

"Insert the syringe, this long, curved syringe."

"He put it inside you?" Sam asked.

"Yes, but he was studying to be a doctor—he was very clinical about it. And I got pregnant on the second try."

She remembered how happy she'd been. It had felt like magic, that it had worked so easily, that she'd done it her way, without compromising. Now Sam was making her feel like she'd done something dirty.

She sighed. "Anyway, Rishi never met Phoenix. When he finished school he had to go back to India right away. And he hasn't been back since. I stopped sending him updates a while back, because I think it was too painful to hear about Phoenix when he really wanted a family of his own. Phoenix asks about him, though, and I do hope they'll meet, someday."

"So you were all on your own for your pregnancy?"

"Yep. Rishi went to a few doctor's visits with me before he left. And my sister came to help with his birth—I had him at home, I think I told you that. I stayed home with him for a few months. I was actually hired on by a school in Hayward a few months into my pregnancy, and then after I had Phoenix I took maternity leave, and was out on disability for a while. I stretched it out as long as I could so that I was getting disability until I quit, when I got the job at Peralta. I felt kind of bad about it, but they the administration were assholes, so I didn't feel too bad."

"You shouldn't feel bad," Sam said. "Phoenix is lucky he had all that time with you. Most of my friends have had to go back to work right away after having their kids. It's super painful for them."

"Yeah, it was pretty sweet to have all that time with him. We bonded really strongly because of that first year together. But then I got the Peralta job and had to put him in daycare. That sucked. The woman who ran the place wasn't great, I was starting a new job, starting teaching, really—that whole time was very stressful for me. And then yeah, ever since then I've pretty much had my hands full with just work and the kid. I never even really had the desire to date. But something shifted recently. Like when I decided to take the writing class I started wanting other things too. And then I met you, and now you're the only thing I want."

Anna took a slug of her cider, nervously glancing at Sam. Sam took the bottle from her and set it in the grass. She pushed Anna down to the blanket, and kissed her.

Transitions #2: The Part

It's hard to write about physical stuff, like skating—stuff you do rather than talk about. This writing shit is hard, you guys! It's easier to write about the shit on the inside than the shit on the outside.

I have to be honest. That's why I'm here, writing to you: to be honest. To be real. In my relationship right now—and you guys, this girl might be the love of my life—I can't really be honest about my transness. Not yet. So I figure this blog is a good place to get that convo going.

Anna says it's the girl me she's falling for. The awesomeness of being with someone of the same sex (it's her first time) isn't something she wants to give up. I get that. It's been a long-ass time since I've felt that way, but I did feel that way, at first. Until I realized that I was more like the guys I hung out with than like any of my girlfriends.

So I'll give her a little time. We need our honeymoon. I'm not gonna push her on this right now.

And anyway, I'm not sure yet who I want to be in the future world. I wish I could just be who-I-really-am, and magically my parts would all fall into place how they should be.

How would I be? Hmmm. My chest is cool, I don't need top surgery. Do I want hair on my chest and face? Not really. I mean, I shave all those annoying little hairs on my face already, why would I want more? I definitely don't need a deep voice. I don't care about all that shit.

I just wish I had a dick. I dreaming of having a dick all the fucking time. For fucking DAYS. Not a strap-on, and not an enlarged clit, but a real dick. Might as well make it a big one, but I'd settle for small.

So gods, if you're listening, this is what I want to be. I want my life, just how it looks now, I want to be who I

am but with just one thing added: a cock.
    If you could add or subtract one thing about you,
what would it be?

PHOENIX

I had my first day of kindergarten today and it was NOT GOOD. You are not going to believe this but George IS at Peralta and he is in MY CLASS. That is the worst thing that ever happened.

The rest of Peralta, which I already knew, is nice. They have gardens, lots of flowers and even vegetables that all the kids and teachers get to water. Not all at the same time, we will take turns. And even the kindergarteners have our own special garden and playground like a secret place for just us where no one else gets to go. It would be good except George is allowed there.

I don't even want to tell you what he did but Mama says it's good for me to talk about it. She is typing this so if I want to tell you I have to tell her. I don't want to, Mama. I already told you at lunchtime.

Lunch was in a big room with lots of tables and grown-ups yelling at us. I didn't like that so much either. We were eating with only the other kindergarten class, which has one friend from my preschool in it so that's good and we got to sit together. His name is Eli and he has brown hair and brown skin and he wears overalls like every day.

The happy thing is the dragon story! It does have a boy in it and his name is Elmer and he and the dragon become friends. Elmer sounds like Eli but when I mentioned it to Eli at lunch he had no idea what I was talking about. So I guess the other kindergarten teacher does not do the dragon story. I am definitely in the right class.

Except George is in my class.

Okay, okay, Mama, I'll tell it. The thing George did is actually two things.

The first thing: He told some kids that I USED TO have accidents at school and then they all called me Pee Pants when we were outside in the special kinder garden. They laughed at this, these three stupid kids and stupid George with his stupid green shirt that says JUST DO IT. Mama says I can always tell a teacher if something like this happens but this was way too embarrassing a story to tell Ms. Rosen on the first day I met her. I didn't want to make her first day terrible too!

The second thing George did was even worse because it will last all year long. He wrote with black marker on a book that I love called *One Fish Two Fish Red Fish Blue Fish*. He knows I love this book because EVERY DAY at preschool I would get this book to read at naptime, until HE started taking it instead. Just so I couldn't! And now the book at my new school is ruined so that I don't even WANT to read it anymore. He made a big black X on the cover of it!

(Note from Mama: Phoenix is having a little cry.)

I'm back. I had to cry, I couldn't help it, because all day I wanted to so much but I didn't. Mama says it's okay to cry at school but there is no way I would let George have that satisfacting that he hurted me.

Mama says this is definitely a lot of bad things for my first day and so it's good I cried. But she also says that maybe George is acting this way because he really wants to be my friend, and I think that is the most ridiculous thing she has ever said. She says you never know, people do bad things sometimes for good reasons.

Whatever! If Skyla was here that's what she would say.

At least George did get in trouble for writing on the

book—a girl called Anya told the teacher on him and he got a timeout. Maybe Ms. Rosen will hate him too.

Aargh! Thinking that he is going to be there tomorrow too, and the day after, and the day after that too, and then next week, and so many more weeks! I don't know what I will do. I have to be good so that I can be in Mama's class next year.

Aaaaaaaaaaaaaaaaaaaaaaaaaaaaaaaaaaaaaaaaaaaaaaaaaa aaaaaaaaaaaaaaah!

Chapter 6

*S*am came for dinner wearing a fedora and carrying daisies. She handed them to Phoenix when he opened the door, and he turned to Anna, his eyes big, and said, "Daisies!"

Anna winked at him, and Sam walked in.

They had decided a few days before that it was time to introduce Sam to Phoenix, and Anna had been nervous ever since. Would he think it was weird that she was with a woman? She had no idea. Since she'd never introduced him to anyone before, maybe it wouldn't be a big deal. What if Sam liked her less once she saw her as a mama? So much of what they had was based on sex and their physicality together, and if Phoenix was there they couldn't have that. Anna didn't know what they would have then.

But Anna had really been struggling with how to help Phoenix with his George issue. She couldn't talk to the parent, or the teacher, because of her position at the school. For the first time she was unable to help him fix his problems. When she told Sam about the situation, Sam said that maybe she could help, maybe it would be easier for her since she wasn't personally involved.

So they had agreed it was time.

Anna introduced them, and put the daisies in a vase. Right away Phoenix took Sam in to show her his room.

Anna turned on some music and opened a bottle of wine, feeling her nervous energy settle into a happiness she hadn't anticipated, a peaceful feeling that all was right in the world.

When Sam and Phoenix emerged from his room, Anna called them into the kitchen. She poured Sam a glass of wine. Then they washed and floured their hands, each got a chunk of dough and a cookie sheet, and worked the dough into a circle. Phoenix did his all by himself; it was more of a square, but no one cared. Then they piled on the cheese—"you can never have too much cheese," Sam said. Then they each added their own ingredients. Phoenix: spinach and mushroom. Sam: spinach, mushroom, and veggie sausage. Anna: mushroom and veggie sausage. It was like first-grade math, Anna thought. 2 + 1 = 3 - 1 = 2.

They put the pizzas in the oven then and set the timer for 10 minutes. The kitchen was small but Anna moved around it gracefully; when her arm brushed against Sam's, a jolt of desire moved through her, and she actually had to grab the counter, afraid she might fall.

Sam asked, "You okay?" and Anna nodded, thinking to herself, *God, I am so sprung.*

They washed the flour off of themselves, set the table, poured some more wine (mango juice for Phoenix), and then the timer went off and they ran to the oven and peered in. The cheese was bubbling, perfectly brown. They pulled the pizzas out of the oven and served up a slice of each pizza for all three of them.

Sitting at the Formica table, Anna looked at their pizza, still steaming, too hot to eat. "Cheers," she said, raising her glass, and they clinked glasses. "Thanks for coming over," she said to Sam.

"Yes," Phoenix agreed, nodding. "I like your hat."

Sam took it off and tossed it across the table, right onto his head.

After they'd eaten, Anna said she'd clean up and Phoenix took Sam by the hand into his room again. She could hear them in there laughing, and she started to feel excluded, like they didn't want her or need her. She had been expecting this to be difficult for Phoenix, or for Sam, but they seemed to be having no problem whatsoever. Instead, it was her who was feeling difficult.

She poured herself some more wine and turned up the music. When she finished the dishes, she went to her room and closed the door. She knew she should be happy that they were getting along so well, but it felt unfair somehow. She'd done all the work raising Phoenix but Sam could just jump in and he would love her instantly? And Sam—she had seemed like Anna's special prize. She didn't want to share her with Phoenix. Not yet.

Maybe they had introduced Sam too early; they should have had more time alone first. Now it seemed like the honeymoon was over, and Anna knew they would never get it back.

She turned on an episode of *The Sopranos*—she had just started watching the series—and tried to ignore the fun she was missing in the other room. She could hear Phoenix's giggles even with her door shut and desperately wanted to know what he was laughing at, but there was no way she was going in there.

After a while her eyes started to fall closed. Just then Sam opened the door and came in, and Anna pretended to be asleep.

"He wants you to read him a book," Sam said.

Anna grunted. "Why don't you do it. You're his new best friend."

"You're not jelly, are you?" Sam asked. "We're buds. You're his mom. Very different."

"I'm not jealous," Anna said. "Just, you know, I spent my twenties raising him. All you have to do is come in here in your fedora and it's on."

"Aw, come on. For real? You're mad? I thought tonight went really well."

"For you," Anna said.

"And for Phoenix! He seems pretty happy."

"Whatever. Why don't you go read to him, before he comes in here wondering what's happening."

"Okay, I will. You rest. You're probably just tired from the wine."

"Am not," Anna mumbled sleepily.

Sam shook her head and left the room, closing the door behind her.

Soon Anna was snoring, her mouth hanging open, *The Sopranos* still killing one another.

In the morning, Anna was contrite. Through her hangover haze she had a vague recollection of how ridiculous she'd acted. She texted Sam an apology, but Sam was at work and didn't write back.

Phoenix came padding into Anna's bedroom, and she said, "Good morning, Paddington." That had been his favorite story when he was little.

"Morning, Mama," he said and climbed up with her. Her bed was high and to get up he had to pull himself up and jump at the same time. She pulled him over to her and held him tight, and he went limp in her arms.

"You okay?" she asked.

"Yep. Where's Sam?"

"She's at work," Anna said. "She didn't sleep here," she clarified.

"Why not?" Phoenix asked.

"Um, we thought it would be better if she slept at her house."

"But why?"

"Well, to keep things simple."

"But things are simple. I like her."

"I'm glad."

"Can we play with her again today?"

"Well, she's at work…"

"Maybe we could bring her some leftover pizza?"

She paused. "That's a good idea, dude. Maybe we could. I've never been there. It's a tattoo studio, you won't be scared of the loud machines?"

"No way! I'm a lot tougher than you think, Mama."

She laughed. "Yes, you are a toughie." They were quiet for a minute. "I'm sorry I didn't read you your book last night."

"That's okay," he said earnestly. "Sam did a good job."

"What book did she read?"

"*Where the Wild Things Are*. She said it was her favorite."

Anna knew it by heart. "The night Max wore his wolf suit and made mischief of one kind…"

"And another!" Phoenix said, and they laughed.

Anna looked at the clock. It was 11. She knew Sam took her lunch break around noon on Saturdays. "Okay, let's do it," she said. She texted Sam again: WE'RE BRING-ING YOU PIZZA.

The shop where Sam worked was on Solano Avenue in Albany, small and more elegant than Anna had expected. When they got there, the owner, Joey—also a butch lesbian, but heftier than Sam—looked up from her book, behind the counter. "Hey!" she said.

"Hey," Anna and Phoenix both replied.

Joey smiled and said, "I know who you guys are."

"You do?" Phoenix asked. "How do you know?"

"Sam told me about you."

"Is she here?" Anna asked.

"Nope, she went to skate. At the Berkeley park. It's not too far from here, down at the end of Fourth Street?"

"We brought her pizza," Phoenix said.

"You should take it over there," Joey said. "I'm sure she'd love to see you. She left her phone at home, but I know she's there, she just left a little while ago."

"Want to come with us?" Phoenix asked.

"No thanks," Joey said, smiling. "Gotta run the shop."

"It's cool," Phoenix said, looking around at the tattoo pictures on the wall.

"Thanks," Joey said. "You should come back sometime when I'm doing a tattoo, or when Sam is. Now *that's* cool."

"I will!" he said. "I would like to!"

"I knew you were tough from the minute I saw you," she said, nodding seriously. "Maybe you'll even want to get a tattoo someday."

Anna started to object, but stopped herself. Joey kept her eyes on the kid.

"Maybe," he said, nodding. "Does it hurt?"

"Nah," Joey said. "Nothing you couldn't handle."

"She's kidding, Phoenix," Anna said. "It hurts a lot."

"You got any?" Joey asked her.

Anna had a feeling that Joey already knew the answer

to that question. She wasn't sure why Joey was challenging her, unless Sam had told Joey about Anna's ridiculous behavior the night before. She shook her head, her cheeks turning red.

"Well, how do you know then?" Joey teased good-naturedly.

"I don't," Anna admitted.

"Well, you come back in and get one too then. Everyone should have at least one."

"Okay," Anna said. "So, the park is at Fourth and what?"

"A block north of Gilman."

"She skated over there?" Anna asked. "That's kind of far."

"She did," Joey said. "She skates everywhere. Faster than her scooter."

"Okay, well, it was nice meeting you," Anna said.

"Nice meeting you!" Phoenix said and stuck out his hand. Joey shook it.

"You too. Enjoy the sun."

"You want a piece of pizza?" Phoenix asked.

"Sure!" she said. "What kind?"

Phoenix opened up the pizza delivery box they'd put the pizza in after they heated one big piece of each pizza for Sam. The cheese was still melty and they all looked at it longingly.

"Wow," Joey said. "No, you better give that to Sam. She's a lucky guy."

"You mean girl?" Phoenix asked.

"No. Sam's really more of a guy."

Anna could see that Phoenix was thinking this over. She didn't want to get into a gender identity discussion here in the tattoo parlor, with her five-year-old and someone who seemed not to like her much. "Okay, well, we better get this over to her! Thanks, and I'm glad we got to meet you." She smiled.

Joey smiled back, looking Anna up and down. She had red lipstick on as always, a short black skirt, and a big PJ Harvey concert T-shirt, with black Converse. "You guys are a pretty cute match. She likes you a lot, you know."

Anna smiled, her blue eyes softening. "I like her too."

"Get out of here then," Joey said, shooing them out.

Chapter 7

*T*hey parked and Phoenix carried the box, both of them craning their necks, searching the curves and valleys of the skate park for Sam. Anna was nervous, seeing all the guys zooming around, and sitting, watching. What if Sam wasn't out here—what if she didn't want Anna and Phoenix showing up and giving her away?

Someone was sitting in their car with the window open, and Anna recognized Neutral Milk Hotel pouring out, which helped a little. She felt like someone in a movie.

She and Phoenix went up to the chain-link fence and she hung on it like a groupie. Just then she saw her. Him. She realized she'd never asked Sam what pronoun she preferred. Joey had called her "her," but she'd also said Sam was a guy. It was all so confusing.

And from above you how I sank into your soul/Into that secret place where no one dares to go…

It was Anna's first time seeing Sam skate. She felt like she was melting, and gripped the chain-link tighter.

Sam was two valleys to the left, and heading toward them. She had her head down, hadn't seen them yet.

"Sa—" Phoenix started.

"Shh," Anna said. "I wanna watch her for a minute."

She had grace, bending into the curves, she made it

look easy. She made it sexy, in her black T-shirt with the sleeves cut off, her tattooed arms at her side looking ready for anything, her black cutoffs tight on her toned legs, the same teal Adidas she'd worn on their first date, easy on the board. Anna could see that she was meant for this.

She sped up a hill and into the air, caught her board below her, and then landed on it, crouched low and dipping again into another valley, fast, fast, Anna couldn't believe how fast, and then up again, a look of concentration Anna had never seen on her before, and she came up out of there and then jumped onto a sliding thing like a sidewalk curb, slid all the way across it, and then she was right next to them and going fast down and out of another hill. Just then, in the air, she saw them, and Anna thought she would fall and her heart stopped but Sam landed smoothly, skidding to a stop and turning around.

Sam skated up to the fence and then came to a sliding stop again, catching her board in the air. "Hey, guys," she said. "What you doing here?"

Anna just stood staring at Sam grinning at her. That sweet face so full of light as she pushed her Ray-Bans up on her head.

Anna felt like she might pass out. *How can she be so fucking hot? How is this my girlfriend? How does she not hate me for being such a baby last night?*

"We brought pizza," Phoenix said, holding up the box. In his excitement, he knocked it against the fence and flew out of his hands. The box opened and as if in slo-mo Anna saw the slices, about to fall out. She dove for it, hitting the box from underneath, the slices again jumping out of the box, above their heads. Anna grabbed the edges of the box with both hands and held it steady at her head, heard the slices land.

Anna's eyes went big. They all three broke into laughter together.

"That was rad," Sam said.

"That was rad!" Phoenix said.

They started walking toward the exit, Sam inside and watching them, Phoenix grabbing a stick and running ahead, stick bumping against the fence as he trailed his hand along it, Anna putting the box in her right hand and moving her left hand up against the fence. Sam did the same with her right. Neutral Milk Hotel was still playing. They stopped and turned to face each other and pulled their faces close, kissing through the fence.

The beauty and frustration of barely being able to kiss, of not being able to touch. The beauty and frustration of love were about equal, most days.

Today, though, Anna thought, the beauty way outweighed the frustration. She was being forgiven for her faults. She ran after Phoenix, toward the gate, toward Sam.

PHOENIX

Mama's new Sam is a skateboarder. She flies through the air! I want her to teach me how.

Mama is shaking her head.

Mama, I would wear a helmet.

She's still shaking her head.

Anyway, Sam is so cool! We brought her pizza at the park where the skaters play, and she said it tasted even better the day after. She was sweating a lot, because it was a hot day and also she was working so hard, with the flying.

Mama just stared at Sam, crying. Mama, why did you cry?

Mama says she cried because she was happy. But I don't understand, if you were happy, then why did you cry?

She is just shaking her head and telling me to focus on my writing.

Okay, so I liked Sam a lot. Mama did a good job of finding someone finally.

Mama's skin looks white. No, Mama, don't write that.

She says she's writing everything I say. She says we need the Dragon thing to do this instead. She has to make dinner.

Okay, good night!

Transitions #3: The Girl

Let me give you an image of Anna, since you don't get to see her like I do. Imagine you are at the skate park. You're sailing up out of a bowl and something catches your eye, something red.

It's her lipstick.

She presses her face to the fence and those lips are framed perfectly in a diamond of chain-link, and you almost miss your landing. Okay and then you skate up to them, her and her kid, much smaller but equally cute, well almost as cute. She is wearing a PJ Harvey T-shirt. She looks like your dream girl from high school.

And she looks at you like you're the king of the world. And she and her boy brought you pizza.

This is what I'm dealing with, you guys. So she's not the most supportive about the trans stuff, not yet. And she worries about me hurting myself skating, gets jealous that I can risk my life while she has to stay unbroken for her kid.

None of that matters. I would do anything for her.

I know it's dangerous. This is how you lose pieces of yourself. It's happened before. My parts grow weak in their sockets and it's easy for people to just pull one free and gnaw on it for a while.

I would happily give her my heart to eat if she asked for it.

You guys, I have to tell you a secret: I love her. I love this girl.

Sam Stray
Creative Writing Assignment #5. Describe a presence—a person, a pet, a piece of furniture, an illness, a secret. Use all five senses.

You would think it would be heavy, but it's lighter than light. It shimmers in its dark place, too bright to live there. It's uncomfortable in the darkness—it wants out. But its owner is too afraid, locks it in for just a little longer. Its bright feathers are so beautiful, but the rustling they make can be loud, can hurt the ears.

It's all about timing. In the wrong light it could wither away, or explode, or maybe it's the owner that might explode if it were to get free. The smell is of wood burning, and to touch it would be hot like fire, but so soft, it's impossible to let go of. It's so sweet you would never want to eat anything else again.

Chapter 8

*A*nna fell asleep on her lunch break the following Monday, curled in a patch of sun on the floor of her classroom. The kids came back from lunch to find her there, and called out, "Ms. Anna, wake up!"

Anna woke, disoriented to find them there, sweating from the sun. "I must have fallen asleep," she said. "Sorry, kids." She rubbed her eyes and sat up. "How long have you been standing there?"

"Not very long, Ms. Anna," said Emmett, his two big front teeth like a bunny's. Most of the other kids had lost theirs, but not Emmett. They looked ready to pop.

The first graders noisily filled her classroom, and Ms. Clark's room next door, the storm after the quiet. Anna remembered that she'd been planning to photocopy their assignment for the afternoon on her lunch break. Instead she'd fallen asleep, which she'd never done at school before. What the hell was wrong with her? Now she'd have to come up with something else for them to do.

She walked to her desk and pulled out a can of green tea, quietly popped it open and took a big gulp, then set it on the desk. She went to the windows and opened them, gazing out and wishing she was out there instead of in here. All she could think of was Sam anyway; she was hopeless.

Phoenix was settled in for rest time by now. She wondered what he'd eaten; she hadn't had time to pack him a lunch that morning so he'd have gotten cafeteria lunch. These days he ate little from his lunch anyway, preferring to go outside and catch butterflies in the garden. George never went in the garden.

She sighed, feeling the pressure of the children behind her, waiting for her. She turned around and saw them all sitting on the rug in a circle, the first time they'd done it on their own. She smiled and said, "Nicely done, kiddos!" She walked to her desk, took another gulp of green tea, popped an Excedrin, and met them on the rug, a video playing in her head of Sam, skating toward her, always skating toward her.

That afternoon Jody from the office came to Anna's classroom and poked her head in, motioning for Anna to come over. When she did, Jody said, "Phoenix is in the office. Something happened. I'm not sure what. He's okay," she said quickly when she saw Anna's already pale face drain even further. "I think he got in trouble, though. I'm not sure what happened, but I wanted you to know."

"Can you watch them?" Anna asked, pointing back at her class, who were looking over curiously.

"You know I can't," Jody said.

"Shit," Anna said. "What should I do?"

"Sit tight," Jody said. "Garcia is handling it. Another hour and you'll be out of here. I'm sure everything will be sorted out by then."

Why did you tell me if I can't do anything about it? Anna thought, shutting the door and heading back to the rug, where the class was free-reading. "Who wants to listen to a book on tape?" she asked. She put on *Frog and Toad Are Friends,* mumbling to herself, "Just friends, my ass." She lay down on the floor with them, unable to fight gravity any longer. They lay on their backs and listened, looking up at the ceiling, where Anna had taped stars and planets, comets and a giant moon.

Anna's head pulsed, and she forced herself not to worry about Phoenix. She closed her eyes and fell asleep again.

George and Phoenix had gotten in a fistfight in the kinder garden. Anna laughed out loud when the principal told her, not believing her at first until she saw that Ms. Garcia was wearing a very unamused look. She pulled Anna aside. "Also, one of your kids just mentioned that you were sleeping during class today. What's going on, Anna? Are you pregnant or something?"

"Impossible," Anna said softly. "I'm sorry, I haven't been sleeping well. Where's Phoenix?"

"At my desk," the principal said, nodding her head toward the back of the office.

"Where's George?" she asked.

"His mom came and got him. He was bleeding pretty bad."

"What?!" Anna laughed nervously.

"I told you, they got in a fight. Phoenix was unstoppable." Garcia shook her head admiringly.

"What the hell?"

"I know. Get in there and talk to him. I think he's a little freaked out. I haven't decided yet what to do about all this. I think I have to suspend him."

"What? No! You can't, I have to teach."

"We'll get a sub."

Anna shook her head, out of words, and headed in to where Phoenix was sitting, drawing, at the desk. He looked up when Anna walked in and held his arms out to her like a teddy bear. She picked him up and held him to her, and he wrapped his legs around her and cried.

Chapter 9

*M*s. Garcia ended up suspending Phoenix for two days, Thursday and Friday. Anna stayed home with him. She didn't punish him. It had been a long time coming—Anna wasn't sorry that George had gotten punched after everything he'd done to Phoenix. She knew George's mom, from the preschool, and that woman seemed to have something not nice in her too. When Anna had tried to talk to her, the year before about the trouble the boys were having, the woman had reacted with an aggression that surprised and scared Anna. And Anna was not easily scared.

Anna tried to talk to Phoenix about what had happened, but Phoenix got so worked up every time he tried to explain it, and there was something about a dragon, and it didn't make any sense. Finally she told herself it didn't matter. She got two days at home with her boy, *and* the weekend. And the timing was good, because her headache had gotten worse.

So they called Sam to come over, and she brought Oxy for Anna, ice cream sandwiches for Phoenix, and marine life documentaries for them all to watch. She told Phoenix, "It feels good, I know, to hit someone when you feel that angry. But after, it always hurts more than it feels good." He stared at Sam, and she pulled him into her chest. Anna watched them, and she thought, *That was what he needed.*

They cuddled together in Anna's bed. After taking a Oxy, Anna felt light, like her bed was a boat. It was just the three of them and the ocean on the screen and that was how she wanted it to be always. She held their hands and fell asleep holding tight to her buoys.

They stayed in Anna's bed for two days, Phoenix and Anna's suspension—for it felt as if she had been suspended too, in solidarity—coinciding with Sam's days off. They ordered food and watched movies and ordered presents for one another online.

When Sam had to go to work on Saturday, they held on to her pant legs and begged her not to go.

"Gotta bring home the bacon," she said in a fake-low voice, and Anna laughed.

"What bacon? We don't eat bacon!" Phoenix said.

"I know, bud. Don't worry, I won't bring home any bacon."

When she said "home" her eyes met Anna's. They were each other's home now. It had happened just like that.

Anna skipped writing class on Wednesday, still fighting a migraine, and Sam brought over the assignment she'd missed. When she had turned in Anna's assignment from the previous week, she said, their professor had raised an eyebrow.

"Looks like our secret's out," she told Anna.

"It was fun being your secret lover."

They looked at each other, longing oozing from their pores. They hadn't had sex in six days.

Anna looked at the kitchen clock. "Only an hour till

his bedtime," she said. "Just sayin.'"

"Plenty of time for me to get ready," Sam responded.

Anna laughed, but Sam didn't. Was she serious?

Sam went into Anna's room, looking back at Anna, dead serious, before she shut the door.

Anna's clit tingled, and she decided to get a head start on putting the boy to bed.

Forty-five minutes later, Phoenix was asleep. Anna removed herself from his bed carefully, tiptoeing out of his room and over to hers. At the door, she knocked quietly. "Come in," she heard from inside. As she opened the door she heard, in a low voice, "Leave the light off."

Anna locked the door and walked toward the bed in the dark, a little nervous. As she reached the bed, she felt something behind her—and then arms were around her, holding her tight like a straitjacket, and a mouth on her neck, and her ear, and something pressing against her ass, like a hard-on.

She was pushed onto the bed, and held there, the body behind her heavy on hers, the mouth on her neck wet and hungry. Anna moaned, and felt her shirt being pulled up but not all the way off, binding her arms and pulling up her hair, so that her back and neck were fully exposed.

It felt unbearable, waiting. Her body bloomed with readiness.

She felt her neck and back begin to be devoured, under her arm, the side of her breast. The wetness traveled down her back, to her ass cheeks. Her skirt was pulled off, and her ass was in the air, and then she felt the most deeply blissful thing she had ever felt, the wetness now inside her, softer than anything she'd never felt.

"Ohhh," she said. It was all she could do or say.

And then she was pushed to the bed again, and there were fingers inside her, and a sound like hers, *Ohhh*, then her wetness was dripping out of her and her legs were being spread and then she was being fucked, up against the edge of the bed, moving to greet the cock as it entered her, slowly at first but she wanted more.

She pushed back harder and harder and the hardness pushed into her harder and harder, her clit hitting the bed. The wetness on her neck, and the sounds, deep and wanting, her hair and arms still caught in her shirt, her entire body exposed. She was giving it all away.

And then she heard and felt from outside herself a building, a coming, that was violent, coming harder and harder and faster and faster until Anna too was coming. She cried out, her screams muffled by the bed, her body exploding into her lover's, her legs quivering, and then Sam pulled out of her and kissed her butt, her back, her neck, her ear, and as she did Anna reached down and touched herself, rubbed hard, and came again.

And then finally, finally, there was a nothingness in her head. No ache, no thought, no sound. Just clear unrippled water and Sam's breath, gentle like the wind on her ear.

PHOENIX

I can write anytime I want now! I talk to the Dragon and it listens to me and writes what I say in the computer. Mama and Sam bought it for me, the Dragon, when we were suspended. I told them it's not good to reward me for bad behavior but Mama said it was good we got suspended because we needed to be with Sam since she's always working on the weekends when we want to hang out with her. Sam said it's never good to hit someone, it will always feel bad after.

She was right. The thing with George was terrible. Terrible, horrible. When I went back to school after I hit him he had a big bandage over one eye and a scary glare with the other eye that was staring on me all day, like an evil eye, which is a kind of spell. I hope he did not put it on me.

It was Saffron that made me to do it. Saffron is my tiny dragon. I can finally tell you about her now—I was worried Mama would think I was crazy if I mentioned her before.

Saffron is the size of my pinky fingernail, so small she can fit in my ear and that is where she stays most of the time. She only comes out if I need her help. Her body is yellow and her wings are red.

Saffron first came to me at preschool, when George and his friends ganged up on me outside when there weren't any teachers there. Saffron said in my ear, "They're just scared boys. You are better than them because you are not scared."

But now that I am in big kid school, Saffron told me I need to stand up for myself. So when George stuck his foot out and tried to trip me and I saw the foot so I didn't fall, Saffron was still mad and she said "Hit him."

And so, I hit him. Well, my hand did. What was weird was that my hand, like, knew what it was doing, whammo right in George's mouth and he actually fell down like in the movies when they do that. I couldn't believe it.

"Nice one," Saffron said in my ear.

So it's funny that this talking typing thing is called Dragon, because I have a dragon too and not only that, my name is Phoenix. They are both mythological creatures, supposed to be, but really real. I mean, if Saffron is real then phoenixes must be real too. It's like how Mama says magic is real, just not everyone can see it or know it.

I want to tell you all this because maybe someday I will meet you, my dad, and I want you to know me then, but it would take a long time to tell you everything. So this way you can know a lot already, about the real things that not everyone knows.

Also, Mama and Sam are spending some quiet time together, so this is something for me to do while they are being quiet without me.

I like Sam very much, but I don't like quiet time. Saffron says I'm not alone because I have her, and the Dragon program too, two dragons actually. Three if you count Elmer from the book. They'll keep me safe tonight.

Anna Harvey
Creative Writing Assignment #7. Imagine an extraterrestrial landed at your workplace. The creature has never been to Earth. Explain it, with as much meticulous detail as you can.

The tall brown rectangle has a small round thing about halfway down—take hold of it, turn, and push. As you walk forward you will hear and see a lot of things all at once: small beings, many of them, tiny humans we call children. They are half the size of a regular human, but twice as loud.

In this room there are thirty-three of them, and instantly they surround you, asking questions, poking you with their fingers, singing, and yelling at you when you don't respond. Look around, and on the walls you'll see more rectangles, smaller ones with lots of colors and shapes—these are expressions the children have made, a representation of what they feel inside.

You'll see a large square in the middle of the floor, with more colors and shapes. If you sit down on it, it will be soft, but I don't recommend this, because the children will surround you until you can barely breathe. No, my recommendation is to go the other way: back to the tall rectangle, pull again on the small circle, and exit the room, leaving the tiny humans behind you.

Chapter 10

*P*hoenix had been sleeping in his own bed for more than a year, but now that Sam was around he didn't want to miss out on the fun. Ever since the suspension, he'd been asking to sleep with Anna, especially when Sam was over.

Anna was feeling a bit pouty about it, wanting her old alone time with Sam back. Wanting sex, all the time. Trying not to resent the kid for making this impossible.

Sam loved it. She had never really cuddled with a kid before, and the sweetness made her happy, softened her in places she hadn't known were hard. The three of them slept together most nights now, mostly at their place during the week, Sam's on the weekend.

Anna and Phoenix liked being at Sam's—it felt like a little vacation. She was gone at work during the days so they walked around Albany, to the bookstore and the Bone Room. They went to the Vivarium to visit the snakes and turtles, went to see Sam skate, brought her lunch. The sun was out and it felt like summer, like it always did in the fall: the Bay Area's delayed reaction. Anna's favorite time of year: the darkness of winter far enough away that she hadn't even started worrying about it yet.

Anna starting thinking about Halloween. She and Phoenix had always done tandem costumes, but now there was a new person in the mix. While they made dinner that night, Anna and Phoenix asked Sam if she liked dressing up for Halloween. Turned out she loved it as much as they did.

"Last year I was a wolf," Sam said. "Oh, I know, Phoenix, you could be Max in his wolf suit! From *Where the Wild Things Are.* If you want you can use my costume."

"Oooh, that's a really good idea," Anna said.

"You guys could be Wild Things," Phoenix said.

"Oh, my god, Phoenix, that's a *really* good idea!" Anna said.

"Yeah, totally," Sam said. "We can have a wild rumpus!"

They got out *Where the Wild Things Are* and thought about what they had that they could wear, and what they would need. Sam made a list as Anna chopped veggies for a salad. Sam had stopped eating meat.

Sam adapted her wolf costume from the year before into a Max costume for Phoenix. It was a gray hoodie covered in light- and dark-gray fur, with ears on top and a tail in the back. She added pipe-cleaner whiskers in the front, and made paws with long black claws. Anna bought him gray sweatpants to match.

They watched the Spike Jonze *Where the Wild Things Are* movie as they carved pumpkins a few nights later, and Anna decided she would be the bird Wild Thing. Sam wanted to be the main one, the big one played by James Gandolfini. She said she had the perfect striped sweater.

"The night Max wore his wolf suit..." Anna said, as Sam unveiled him on Halloween night, at her place. It was a novelty, not having to do all the work of outfitting him for the first time this year—though it was work Anna loved, the surprise was pretty sweet. Phoenix came out in his wolf suit and posed, holding up his paws with a fierce look on his face. As Anna took pics with her phone, Phoenix channeled his inner wild one, jumping up onto Sam's couch, over to an armchair, then off and onto her white rug. Anna tried not to worry about the (comparatively) fancy furniture in Sam's place.

Next Sam went into her bedroom and came out wearing the stripy sweater, horns atop her messy black wig. She did the fierce paws-raised thing next to Phoenix, and made a face like him. They growled at each other, and Anna took more photos.

Then Anna snapped her beak on her face. It was big and yellow and looked just like the Wild Thing in the movie, but the rest of her costume was pretty basic: furry cream-colored hoodie and some snakeskin-looking pants.

Sam said, "Hold on, I'll be right back," and disappeared out the back door.

Anna said, "And now…let the wild rumpus start!" Anna and Phoenix danced to the Le Tigre record playing as Sam came back with her arms full of white feathers.

"One of my drag queen clients paid me in feathers," she said. "You mind if I glue these onto your hoodie?" she asked Anna.

"Go for it," Anna said, stopping her dancing and kneeling in front of Sam, giving her a wink that Phoenix couldn't see, remembering the week before, when Anna had knelt before Sam and given her what she called "the best blowjob of my life."

Sam assembled a kind of Mohawk with the feathers as Phoenix jumped around the house, imitating the creatures he saw.

When all the feathers were glued on Anna's hood, they gave them a few minutes to dry and then headed out. The sun was just going down. Sam left a bowl of candy on her porch for the trick-or-treaters and lit the candles in their pumpkins.

They piled into the Prius and headed toward the party the tattoo parlor was hosting. Anna took off her hood in order to fit in the passenger seat. She put the beak up on top of her head and, in the mirror, put on her trademark red lipstick—even as a Wild Thing. She smiled over at Sam in the passenger seat, and Sam blinked her long, furry fake eyelashes at Anna suggestively.

Anna laughed and turned to look back at Max. "Ready?" she asked Sam and Phoenix as they headed down the hill.

"Yeah!" they yelled in stereo.

"Let's go see some shit," Anna said.

"Mama!" Phoenix said.

"Sorry, dude," Anna said, laughing.

Day of the Dead was even better. It always was.

They got ready at Phoenix and Anna's house this time. Sam did their makeup. With all the skulls she'd tattooed in her life, she was an expert.

First she painted all three of their faces white. Next, she smudged big black circles around their eyes.

It was like they were all three dying, together. A dead little family.

Phoenix's crosshatch mouth turned up at the ends in a smile. On his forehead Sam painted a spiderweb, since he loved spiders, and on his chin an orange sun, his favorite color. He had dressed himself, in his rainbow butterfly wings and a skull-covered pajama top Anna had forgotten about.

Anna was wearing a heavy black shawl, embroidered with flowers all along the back, and a long black skirt that skimmed the ground. Sam had made her a wreath of marigolds, and she painted Anna's face with great care, covering every inch with curlicues, hearts, crosses, and flowers. Anna sat quietly, loving the feel of the brushes on her face, the crown of her head tingling. She adored the focus on Sam's face, like when she skated, the inspiration in her eyes.

"I've never seen you work," Anna realized aloud.

"You haven't," Sam said. "You should come in sometime. You should let me work on you."

"I should," Anna murmured, marveling yet again at her good fortune, finding this incredible creature to love. Or maybe it was karma, her reward for focusing on Phoenix for all those years, being good.

When she looked in the mirror she saw a new self—decorated, decadent. Dark and dead but also ethereal, magical.

Sam's face appeared over her shoulder, white-faced and black-eyed but not yet embellished. "You like?" she asked.

Anna said, "I love." Then she added "you." It was the first time she'd said it.

Sam placed the crown of marigolds on her head, checked its placement in the mirror, met Anna's eyes there, and mouthed "I love you," her first time too. They smiled at each other in the mirror, the happiest of the hundreds of skeletons they would see that night.

Transitions #4: Pronouns

I don't really care what you call me, as long as you're respectful. Here in the Bay Area, most people get that I'm in-between. They understand, and most don't have any problem dealing with it.

Traveling is another story, though. To be honest, it's one reason I don't travel that much.

I appreciate being asked what pronoun I prefer, I just don't really have a strong preference one way or another. Because I don't feel straight up like a girl OR a guy. I feel like something else.

What ze fuck? you may be asking.

Obviously I care about language. I care about the struggle. Of course I believe everyone has the right to write their own story and express their own identity. It's just that I choose my battles, and respect wins out over pronouns for me.

I want respect as a skater. I want respect as a lover. I want respect as a tattoo artist. I don't really want to be a woman OR a man—and I want respect for that. I want respect as a queer person, and now as a parent. That's what I expect, what I ask for.

I'm a skater, you guys. Verbs are just way more interesting to me than pronouns.

Chapter 11

*O*n the day before Thanksgiving, they were driving down to Southern California, to Sam's mom's place. Sam was driving Anna's packed Prius; Phoenix and Anna were both asleep as they started up the Grapevine in the last of the sun.

The lurch of the Prius woke Anna, and she blinked. "Sorry," she mumbled. "Left you alone." She was so sleepy lately, and being driven was yet another novelty. Her system seemed to be letting this new support Sam was providing seep deep into its depletion.

"No prob, dude," Sam said. She'd been listening quietly to New Order. "I'm in my happy place."

Anna smiled at her, disoriented in the almost dark. "I'm glad you have a little light for the Grapevine," she said softly. It had always been her least-favorite part of the trip home, both because the steep grade was such a pain in the ass, especially in the Prius, which had no power—and because it meant they were almost there. The few times she'd been back to see her mom after leaving home had all been hideous.

Anna said quietly, "This drive makes me think of my mom. Not great memories."

"I'm sorry, sweetie," Sam said. "This time will be different. You're gonna love my mom."

Anna turned around to make sure Phoenix was still asleep and hadn't heard what she'd said. He had recently stopped needing a booster seat and he looked so small to her, and so vulnerable with only a seatbelt to protect him. The back seat was covered with his books. He couldn't read them yet on his own, but she knew he would be able to soon. The door would open, and he would walk in.

Sam and Anna had grown up not that far from each other, but Sam's childhood seemed to Anna like it took place on another planet. Sam spoke of her mom like she was a divine being. She did say that high school had been hard, for all of them—back then Sam's dad had been around too. Now he was in a home, with Alzheimer's. Sam hadn't seen him in years.

She'd told Anna that she regretted the shit she had done and said to her mom in high school. She was ashamed of how she'd treated her mom in high school; she'd been pretty bad into drugs and alcohol back then. Her mom had tried to help her, and Sam had treated her like shit. She couldn't forgive herself for it.

Anna looked over at her, remembering Sam's voice breaking when she told Anna this, late one night in bed. She'd thought maybe Sam was about to cry in front of her. It would have been the first time.

But no. Anna had been disappointed. She herself had cried in front of Sam once, after getting jealous a few weeks before when she saw a sexy octopus design Sam was drawing for some woman's ass. "It sucks!" Anna had said, not even aware of her pun. "You're not just looking at other women's asses, you're not just looking at them naked and close up...you're designing fucking artwork for them!" Sam had tried not to laugh or smile, but she couldn't help it, and Anna was so frustrated she'd started to cry.

Sam was focused on the road now, her face spotlighted by the other cars as they passed, falling back into darkness when they were gone. Anna marveled again at how different Sam's face looked in profile, like a whole other person. Sharp, when she was looking at the rest of the world; soft when she looked at Anna.

After they made it up the Grapevine, Sam started reminiscing.

"When I graduated high school I moved in with this friend of mine, a guy I skated with. He had a friend who was a tattoo artist, and I worked in their shop sometimes. Whatever was needed, running out for food, sweeping, taking out the trash. After a year or so the owner of the shop offered me a full-time job, cleaning up and making appointments.

"Over time they taught me how to tattoo. I practiced on myself—little stuff like this." She wagged the heart and lightning bolt on her left pinky and ring fingers. "After a while, the artists let me practice on them. By the time I was twenty I was a full-time tattoo artist.

"My mom was disappointed that I never went to college, but she was happy to have me around, happy I was off drugs and had work I cared about. She'd always supported my artwork. She even hired me this great private art teacher in junior high."

In her early twenties, Sam said, she worked at the tattoo shop and skated with her friends, all guys. She was the only female skater she knew back then. But after a while, though she was open with them about being queer, she said it got kind of old being around these guys who were kind of homophobic. Small-minded, at least. The girls in the scene, she said, were pretty shallow too. "Orange County," she said. "Huntington is cool, but it's still Orange County."

Sam visited San Francisco and fell in love. With the city, and with a girl: the roommate of the friend she stayed with. "I'm such a cliché, I know," she told Anna. She started coming up every weekend, and looking for tattoo jobs, and after a few months she found one, at a shop in the Mission.

She moved in with her girlfriend and her friend the following weekend. Pretty soon she and the girlfriend got their own place, where they lived for the next two years—until Sam found out that her girlfriend had been sleeping with an ex-boyfriend on the sly for one of those years. "That part was cliché too: bisexual girlfriend who's still hooking up with her ex, who's a guy. I learned that one the hard way."

Anna looked; still no tears. "What was her name?"

"Tammy. We were Tammy and Sammy, so dorky. Everyone called me Sammy then. My mom still does."

"Aw, Sammy," Anna said. "I'm sorry Tammy fucked you over."

"Yeah," Sam said, nodding. "I don't know where she is now. We never really talked again after she moved out. That was a pretty rough time for me, living by myself in the Mission. When I moved to the East Bay it was better because I wasn't afraid I'd see her every time I left the house.

"I came down here a lot around that time. I'd skate pools with my high school boys, and my mom would cook for me. My mom's food is hella good. You'll see. And I told her you're veggie—we're veggie—so she's skipping the turkey."

"Are you serious? My family's never done that for me." On Anna's last visit home, her mom had served steak and a salad of iceberg lettuce and nothing else. Anna had filled her plate with lettuce and eaten it slowly, methodically. Her mom had not seemed to notice or care.

"Serious. We'll have lots of great veggies, and stuffing

and gravy are easy to make veg."

"And don't forget my nut loaf!"

"How could I forget your nut loaf?" Sam looked over at her, raising her eyebrows suggestively, and Anna laughed.

Quietly, Sam said, "We're gonna need to find some time alone. I wish we could pull over to the side of the road right now."

"I know. Where will we sleep?"

"In my old room? I don't know, actually. We have a guest room, but Phoenix probably wouldn't want to sleep in there alone, right? I guess we could all sleep in there. It's probably more comfortable, but my room's cooler."

"We'll be there soon," Anna said as they passed the 101. "I'm nervous."

"My mom's gonna love you guys," Sam said assuredly. "Don't worry. She's totally chill. And she loves kids. She was a pediatric nurse, you know, until she retired last year. She's been dying for me to have a kid, so she's gonna be stoked."

Meeting Sam's mom was a revelation. First and foremost: the way Sam was around her. It was like now that she was safe at home with her mom she could let go and be soft, vulnerable, even childish. She kept falling into her mom in a kind of trust fall/hug, her much-smaller mother widening her arms to catch/receive her.

When Olivia mentioned that she had named her daughter Samuelle after her best friend growing up, who was now a well-known bridal dress designer, Anna said she'd never heard this story. Olivia immediately pulled out her iPad and showed Anna the Samuelle Couture website. They'd only been there five minutes and they were gathered at the kitchen table *oohing* and *aahing* over exquisitely delicate wedding dresses that looked like they had been designed for fairies, or ghosts. Anna fell in love with one, the Cecile, which featured a lacy bodice in silk satin, with a simple skirt of tulle and chiffon.

For the first time in her life, Anna imagined herself wearing it. Marrying Sam.

Sam put her arm around Anna and pulled her into her lap, nuzzling her head into her neck, her shoulder, like a happy cat. Phoenix was in Olivia's lap already.

The vision dispersed. No nuptials were needed; the picture was already complete. They had been starting to feel like a family to Anna, in Oakland, but now, here with Olivia, it was official. This felt solid, legit. Unbreakable.

Olivia was much shorter than Sam, and her hair was lighter, but their faces were the same. "Sammy got her mom's face and her dad's body, lucky her," she said, laughing, and it was true, she *was* lucky. Olivia had the same face Anna had fallen in love with. Her heart melted a little every time she looked at Olivia, looking back at her: the now-familiar feeling of the softness in her face being there because she was looking at Anna.

Anna felt so happy, suddenly, it was painful. Like a mini heart attack, or anxiety attack: a pain in her chest. She got up and asked for the bathroom, and when she got there she looked in the mirror and saw her own mom's face there.

She started to hyperventilate, then, seeing the person she hated most, more and more apparent in her the older she got. The claustrophobia of it, that there was no escape from her, made her want to rip her face off.

Anna fought for breath. The distance between what had happened to her then and what was happening to her now felt unsurmountable. She sat on the toilet lid and looked up, at ivy-covered walls, lit by fairy lights, pretty purples and pinks. It was charmed, this bathroom, this life, and she wanted it. She put her hands on her knees and forced herself to breathe deep and slow.

There was a clawfoot tub. She slipped her Converse off and climbed in, the full skirt of her dress—yellow-and-black striped, with a white Peter Pan collar—spreading out around her. She wished she could take a bath. Her body longed for the immersion of self, oblivion, a cleansing of this darkness.

She imagined it instead, and finally she calmed down. She climbed out of the tub, flushed the toilet, and returned to her family.

Chapter 12

*A*nna walked out of the bathroom and saw Olivia in the kitchen. "I'm making tea," she called to Anna. "Want some?"

The kitchen was yellow, with yellow-and-white gingham cabinets. More plants, their leaves covering the walls by the window. She went to the window and fingered a lace curtain that reminded her of the dresses they'd been looking at.

"Auntie Sam made those too, when Sammy was in my belly. She's Sam's godmother."

"What a wonderful gift," Anna said, marveling at the curtains. *They're the same age as Sam. Extra soft around the edges.* "Can I help?"

"Just making a pot of decaf chai, if that sounds good. Sam wants a beer."

"Can I have both?" Anna asked.

Olivia smiled. "Of course! And what about Phoenix, what does he like? We could make cocoa?"

"Oh, my god, he'll love you forever."

"You grew up near here, right?"

"An hour or so inland. But it felt like another world. Let's just say it's nice to be in a warm home."

"I hear you have a very warm home, up in Oakland. Sam likes it a lot, and she's bit of a snob. But she's got good taste."

"She said the same about you," Anna said as she took out two beers. "I'll take this to her."

Anna went back into the other room, where Sam and Phoenix were playing a hand-smacking game. "Who's winning?" Anna asked.

Sam held up her hands like injured paws. "He is."

"He's hurting you or he's hurting your pride?" Anna popped open both beers, handed one to Sam, and clinked it.

"Both." Sam held the cold bottle to her hands in turn, making Phoenix laugh.

"Phoenix. Olivia is making you cocoa."

"Omigod!"

"I know. I'm having chai AND beer! We are so lucky right now." Anna beamed at Phoenix and he smiled back at her.

And then, suddenly, she saw something she had never seen. Her own face smiling back at her. Darker-skinned and younger, but the smile was the same. The same curves, the same light in the eyes.

"Sam, take a picture of us?" Anna said, tears starting in her eyes. She pretended to fix her hair so she could wipe her eyes.

Sam grabbed her Leica from her bag and took a photo of Anna and Phoenix, grinning as big as their faces would hold. Then Sam held the camera out and took one of the three of them.

Sam said, "Come on, let's get one with Mom too!" Anna and Phoenix followed her in as Sam propped the camera on a counter, then ran over and collected everyone in a hug just as the little red light went off.

When they went out to the patio to drink their beverages, they could smell the ocean.

"Can we go to the beach?" Phoenix asked.

"Sure," Olivia said. "We can go after this, if you guys want."

"I want," Anna said.

"Huntington is nice," Sam said. "You can have a fire down there."

"Can we do that?" Phoenix asked. "I always wanted to."

"Fine by me," Olivia said.

"Yes!" Sam said, hugging her mom from behind. "When I was young," she told Phoenix, "I used to walk to the beach barefoot. Till I started skating. Then I needed shoes."

"And shoes, and shoes, and more shoes," Olivia said.

"It must have been handy being a nurse," Anna said to Olivia.

"Yes, so I could stich her back up."

"Have you seen her skate?"

"Of course. Not in a while, though."

"I brought my board," Sam said. "The new one."

"Let me see it," Olivia said, and Sam went to get it.

She came back and handed the new longboard to her mom, then put a smaller board on the ground next to Phoenix, with a helmet and some pads. "I found this in the garage. It's my first board. If it's okay with your mom you can try it out," Sam said to Phoenix. "It's pretty solid, Anna. We would take it slow."

"You want to, Phoenix?" Anna asked, her stomach turning.

He nodded, his eyes lit up bright.

"Alright!" Sam said. "We'll skate to the beach. I can teach you too if you want, honey!"

Anna's eyes got big in a no-thank-you way, and she went inside.

"How's the cocoa?" Olivia asked.

"It's hot," Phoenix said as Anna came back out and put his hoodie on him.

"Blow on it," Sam said.

Anna pulled a flannel on over her dress. Sam patted the loveseat next to her, and Anna retrieved her cup and saucer, and sat.

"Try your cocoa now, Phoenix," Sam said, and he did. He came back up with a giant smile.

It turned out Phoenix wasn't much of a skater, at least not yet. But Anna wasn't half-bad. Well, maybe *half*-bad.

Olivia and Phoenix walked on the sidewalk holding hands while Sam and Anna went on ahead, Anna trying her best not to fall as she laughed, the kids' helmet on her head way too small. Sam skated up next to her, hair blowing into her eyes. She leaned over to kiss Anna, then pushed away again sexily, her willowy body leaning into the wind.

"This is nice," Sam said, holding her hand for a moment before Anna lost her balance, almost falling off the board, then catching herself with steadying from Sam.

"I think I need some more direction," Anna said. "This is kind of hard."

"Skating is hard, dude! It's hard at the beginning. Well, tricks are always hard. But cruising gets to be second-nature. It's just transportation."

And then they were there. They crossed the street, and sat on a low wall bordering the beach, which was lively with locals and tourists on the holiday weekend.

"We can get wood here," Sam said. "I have some cash. I also brought us some beers."

Anna took off the helmet and looked across the street just as Phoenix and Olivia crossed, running against the light during a break in traffic. They saw Sam and Anna and kept running—toward them, toward the sea.

They scored a firepit and Sam started on the fire. Phoenix and Anna looked for kindling, and Olivia spread out a blanket. The sky was glowing with the last of the sun.

There were a few other small groups of people, and even a few people still in the ocean, Anna saw. A couple surfers. She pulled off her sneakers.

Sam took a bottle out of her shorts, opened it, and offered it to her mom, who took it, shaking her head at Sam. Sam opened another and handed it to Anna after she returned with sticks. Then she opened the last one, and they all cheersed.

"Where is Phoenix?" Olivia asked suddenly.

Just then Phoenix came running up and crashed into Olivia on the blanket.

"There he is!" Anna said. She warmed her hands over the fire. "It's great here," she said to Sam. "You're great. And your mom's great too."

"Told you. She loves you guys already."

"We're so lucky," Anna said as she sat down on the blanket with Olivia and Phoenix, who crawled over to sit in his mama's yellow-and-black-skirted lap.

She tickled him. He giggled and squirmed and when she stopped said "Again!"

When Olivia took over the tickling, Anna lay down on her back and turned to where Sam knelt in front of the fire. She pushed herself up on an elbow, took a sip of her beer.

My girlfriend is tending the fire, Anna thought.

Sam's face was lit up by the flames, and her face looked quiet, like she was listening to them.

Transitions #5: Mary Oliver and Olivia Stray

Instructions for living a life:

Pay attention.
Be astonished.
Tell about it.

—Mary Oliver, "Sometimes"

My mom has a magnet on her fridge with this poem on it. I used to not really get it, my eyes would skim over it but I didn't really understand. I think I even felt a little annoyed by it. Maybe I was trying *not* to pay attention, those years when I lived with her, and even when I would visit. I was trying to survive the vibe in Orange County, which meant ignoring a million micro-aggressions a day—and worse, unignorable things like racism.

But now, suddenly, I'm paying attention. I am astonished at my life, and I want to tell you all about it.

My girl skated with me in my hometown over Thanksgiving! She met my mom and they fell in love. The boy came too, and I fell in love with him. He has this epic smile, and eyelashes like a giraffe. He laughs all the time and makes up crazy stories and is fucking hilarious.

It was so warm and cozy in my mom's house. And you know, there were a lot of times when it was not all that warm and cozy up in there. That my mom somehow forgave me for all of the blood and drugs and pain is one of the great miracles of my life.

So today I want to say thank you to Mary Oliver, and thank you to my mom, Olivia Stray. My hero.

Sam Stray

Final Assignment. Write a creation myth, a story that explains some aspect of who you are or how you came to be, in the form of a folk tale or a fairy tale. 500 words.

How the Peacock Got Its Feathers: A Folk Tale
The ancients tell tales of a peacock with a body of brown feathers, like a female, and a train of showy blue-green feathers, like a male.

The peacock wasn't born that way, it was said. When the peahen chick was born, her little body, like all of her siblings', consisted of fluffy light-brown feathers, and her back feathers were darker-brown, mixed with white. As her brothers got older, they grew blue feathers on their neck, while the peahens' neck feathers turned green. Their second summer, after molting, her brothers started to develop both blue and green feathers in their tails.

The peacock was terribly jealous of her brothers. She too wanted the vibrant plumage they strutted. She too wanted to be able to attract the attention of a female.

Day and night, she prayed for the same iridescent train. She practiced prancing, like her brothers did, when none of the other birds were watching.

Summer came, and the birds' hormones caused them to molt. For a short time the peacocks and the peahens looked almost the same, except for the colors at their chests: the females' still green and the males' blue. The peacock noticed, however, that her own scruff was both: a beautiful, shiny blue-green.

She kept a close watch on her tail feathers as they returned. The first few were brown, as usual, and the peacock's heart sank in disappointment. But then, one day, where formerly it had been a dull brown, a tail feather shimmered bright and vibrant in the sun's light. And then another!

The eyes on the feathers were the same green-blue as her chest feathers. But no one else seemed to notice them. Though she was terribly proud, she knew that maybe this was a good thing.

The peacock kept her secret feathers to herself, shaking them out when she was alone and admiring their vibrancy. Her sisters would be angry if they knew, and already she had a hard enough time surviving in the muster, since she was so different from the other females.

In the peacock's third year, when it was time to breed, she worried what would happen. She didn't want to mate with a male, or get pregnant, or have babies, but she also knew that her plumage was nowhere near magnificent enough to earn her the attention of a peahen. The peacock considered leaving the muster, but she knew she would die of loneliness if she did—a fate that had befallen other rebels who left the roost.

She decided to make herself useful. When her sisters needed a break, she offered to sit on their eggs for them. Since the eggs needed constant body warmth, the peacock's services soon became very much in demand, and she moved from nest to nest, as needed.

The next summer, after molting, more blue-green feathers grew. Now almost one quarter of the peacock's feathers had the brilliant teal eyes.

Each year, the peacock's train became thicker, more colorful, and more beautiful. The small blue-green feathers on her chest grew into long blue-green feathers, but the rest of her neck and head remained brown, unlike the males'.

She loved the way she looked, and the way she felt. She loved the earthy brown of her chest, and she loved the showy teal of her tail: that special combination of blue and green that only she had been graced with. Only she got to be all the colors at once.

Chapter 13

*A*nna and Sam decided to dress up for their writing class holiday party, which was also their coming-out as a couple. Sam wore a black button-down with brown wool pants and suspenders, Anna a calf-length burgundy dress that wrapped around her body, her hair twisted up around her head. Dark wine lipstick, earrings a burst of beads and feathers. She brought a Chinese jacket for Phoenix to put on over his school clothes after they picked him up.

The party was at a downtown Berkeley pizza place/brewery, Jupiter, on their back patio. The sun was just going down as they parked, and the three of them walked in holding hands. When they got there, the pizza had just arrived. They were handed plates and slices, and Sam ordered them two IPAs.

As Sam and Anna sat down together, a couple of their classmates smiled.

"You guys look good together," their teacher said.

"You look like you've always been together," said Jules, the sole high school student in their class. He was so talented, he made Anna wish she had started writing sooner.

Jules sat down near Sam, saying, "Hey dude, I wanted you to know, I like your blog."

Sam glanced at Anna, panic in her eyes.

"Your blog?" Anna asked, the words catching in her throat.

"Um, yeah. I put it up a little while ago. Sorry I didn't tell you."

"Oh, I'm sorry." Jules held his hands up in apology. "I just wanted to thank you. It's been really good for me to read some of the stuff you've posted."

Jules, Anna now realized, was trans. He retreated, almost tripping over a planter.

"I thought your blog was gonna be about skating," Anna said.

"It is," Sam said. "But I write about other stuff too."

"When did you put it up?" Anna asked quietly. Phoenix was playing with the child of one of their classmates, driving Hot Wheels through the patio fountain. The rest of their classmates were busy chatting. "Why didn't you tell me?"

"I'll show it to you right now if you want," Sam said, and Anna remembered Olivia pulling out her iPad to show them Sam's namesake within minutes of their meeting.

"No, I don't want to see it." She did really want to see it, but she did not want to tell Sam that. "I want you to explain this to me."

"Hang on a sec." Sam asked their classmate, the one with the kid Phoenix was playing with, if she would keep an eye on him for a few minutes. The woman said of course, and Sam gave a wave to Phoenix, calling out, "Be right back, dude." When he seemed fine with that, waving back happily with a Hot Wheel in his hand, Sam took Anna's hand and led her out of the restaurant, finishing her beer and setting it on the bar as they walked out onto the busy sidewalk.

Anna pulled her hand away now, shaking her head. The

headache that had been lurking in the shadows all day settled in to stay.

They walked down Shattuck. The Christmas lights were lit on the trees, along the side of the road and in the middle divider. Giant red balls hung from the branches.

This should be romantic, Anna thought as she looked at Sam, who had stopped and turned Anna to face her.

Sam said, "Baby. I have been wanting to tell you about this. It's just… At first I was afraid because I thought you wouldn't get the trans stuff."

"Why?"

"Remember you told me you wouldn't want to be with a guy again?"

"Yeah…"

"That made me feel like I couldn't be honest with you about the part of me that's a guy."

"Oh."

"But that was just at first. We were just getting together…."

"It's been up that long?? What is it called?"

"Transitions. Like, in skating, transitions are when you go from horizontal to vertical, like in a bowl or a pool. And you know, being trans, transitioning from being a guy, to being a girl, which is kind of what I do all day long."

"Nice name," Anna had to admit. TRANSITIONS pulsed in '80s neon in her mind.

"Thanks. Anyway, then I wrote a blog post about how I loved you, and I was too embarrassed for you to see it since we hadn't said it yet."

"Oh, my god. I want to see it."

"I'll show you when we get home. Are you mad?"

They were on the island in the middle of Shattuck where they had first eaten ice cream together.

"This is our spot," Sam said, stopping in the middle of the crowd of people and putting her arms around Anna. "Can I kiss you?" she asked.

And Anna said yes.

Chapter 14

*B*ut Anna *was* mad. When she looked at the blog, she loved it, but she felt jealous. Jealous that Sam had done this big thing completely without her, jealous that she'd started writing seriously before Anna had. Even Phoenix had started writing before her! They both had their projects that Anna wasn't a part of.

She felt how much she had invested in Sam. She felt like a snail without its shell. She'd let herself get too soft.

Anna's least-favorite part of her job was teaching math. Every time she stood at the front of the class to teach even just first-grade addition and subtraction, she was reminded of the embarrassing math anxiety she'd had her whole life. When she was a kid, her mom had been unable or uninterested in helping with homework, her dad was always away or working, and her sister was too young to be of any help. Anna had struggled for hours on her own, often literally unable to make the numbers work. It was a language she couldn't understand, a code she couldn't break.

She stood at the white board and put on a fake smile, went to choose a dry-erase marker.

The next thing she knew, she was on the floor, and the

teacher from next door was squatting over her, pushing back Anna's students, who were crowding around, asking "Ms. Anna, are you okay?"

"What happened?" Anna asked the other teacher, whose name was Marie, Ms. Martin to the kids. When she tried to sit up a headache struck like lightning, cracking her brain open. She lay back down and looked up at the ceiling. Little worried faces looked down at her from above.

"Kids, I told you to go sit on the rug!" Marie said sharply. As they dispersed reluctantly, she quietly told Anna, "I think you had a seizure. Jonah ran and got me. When I got here you were twitching on the floor, and then after a minute or so you stopped. How do you feel?"

"Not good," Anna said.

"I can take your class this afternoon," Marie said. "Why don't you go home?"

"Are you sure?" Anna asked. "Sixty-six kids?"

"It'll be fine," Marie said. "I've got a parent coming in. I'll take them next door, you take your time getting up. Do you need anything?"

Anna shook her head as she looked at the other teacher, too scared to be grateful. As soon as the kids were gone a tear leaked out the side of her eye. What was happening?

At home, Anna lay down in bed. Her body felt totally drained but panicky, her limbs twitching like they were electrified. Her head too, throbbed insistently.

She rolled over on her side and checked her bedside table: seven Xanax left, from the depression last year. She was glad now that she had made herself save them.

She popped one, and a couple aspirin, and within a few minutes she felt calmer. *It was just the math,* she told herself, then laughed out loud. "Ha!" she said loudly to the empty bedroom.

She looked at the clock. In five hours she would have to pick up Phoenix from afterschool. She set her alarm for 4:15 and let the meds pull her under.

When the alarm went off, Anna was confused. It took her a long time to remember why she was in bed in the middle of the day.

Then she remembered. The seizure. The pills. She'd been asleep for four hours.

What is happening to me?

She got up and as she did the terrible headache attacked again. She braced herself on the bed, afraid of passing out or seizing up again. She downed a couple more aspirin and the rest of the water by her bed.

Very slowly, she made her way into the kitchen, where she put a piece of bread in the toaster.

This is the first thing I'm eating all day, she thought. *Maybe that's all it is. I need to eat.*

She sat at the bar, sprinkled some cinnamon and sugar on her toast, switched on the electric teapot. A half-hour till she needed to be back at Peralta to get Phoenix.

A little instant coffee would help.

You can do it.

Sam was working, and even if she could get away from the studio, she was too far away to pick him up in time.

You can do this. You have to.

On the drive there, the headache took up a dark residence in her, evading the meds with no problem. Anna drove the mile and a half to the school slowly, in the right lane, ready to pull over if another seizure hit, barely able to see, her right eyelid drawn down halfway.

She parked on the side street at the back entrance of the school. The murals painted there throbbed with a violent, blinding geometry, making her feel like she was on a bad drug trip. Anna looked down and walked, step by step, to the afterschool portable.

The afterschool teachers were alarmed by her appearance; they said she looked like a ghost. She told them not to worry and signed Phoenix out, keeping her head and body very still. She motioned to him to come, and he did, right away. She saw that he was afraid too when he saw her.

He held her hand as they walked out of the portable. She saw that he was watching her, but when she moved her head to look at him, a kind of vertigo started. She squeezed his hand and stared straight ahead.

"Mama, what happened? Some kids said you fell."

Little fuckers, Anna thought. "Honey, you don't need to worry about me. I just got a little dizzy, that's all. I'm gonna get us home and order a pizza. Then I'll go to bed, and I'll be better in the morning. Okay?"

He looked at her skeptically.

"Don't worry," she told him. "Everything's going to be fine."

PHOENIX

My mama is asleep and I am a little afraid but I don't want to wake her up so I am going to talk to you instead. My "audio transcription software," is what the little box I am supposed to click on says when it opens. In the little box is a picture of a dragon, which must be you. I will call you Mr. Dragon.

I have another dragon too, called Saffron. You and Saffron would probably get along good. She is tiny, the world's tiniest dragon, I think.

I don't have any idea how big you are. Well, the size of you in the box I click on is the size of Saffron. Maybe you are her? I don't know. I don't know anything.

My mama fell down at school today. Some big boys told me she crashed down. And when she picked me up she looked so white, and she was walking like in zombie tag.

She got home and right away ordered a pizza, and paid for it with her numbers on the phone. When it got here I answered the door by myself and got the pizza. I even got plates down and put a piece on a plate for her but when I brought it to her she said, "No, thank you." She said she just needed to lie down and was I okay and I said yes. I really wanted to ask could we call Sam but I had to pretend like I was a big boy and not scared so Mama could rest.

Now it's dark and I don't like it in the dark. I turned on a light, that's better. The clock says 8:10 so maybe I should get in bed.

I guess I can have a cookie or two. I can eat them in bed, that's a good thing. Most times Mama says no eating in bed, but I think this time she will understand.

Chapter 15

*A*nna called Ms. Garcia that night, after ordering the pizza, and said she wouldn't be in the next day. "It's just a migraine," Anna told her. "I'll be back Monday."

But in the morning she felt worse, not even well enough to drive Phoenix to school. It was too early to call Sam and ask her to take him, and it was too far of a drive, too much to ask. Anyway Anna didn't want to worry her. She asked Phoenix to turn on a movie for himself and pour a bowl of cereal.

Then she vomited. The first time in a decade or more. It was terrible, like all those years of toxicity were erupting out of her, and she didn't feel better afterward like people always said. She felt completely drained. She lay down in their tiny bathroom and fell asleep in there.

Phoenix went into the bathroom to pee and found her there. "Mama! Why are you sleeping here?"

"Oh, Phee, I just felt tired so I lay down and, whoops! Fell asleep! Are you okay, are you hungry? There's leftover pizza."

"I'm okay, thanks," he said politely. "Should we call Sam to come help us?"

Anna looked at him, in his red footie jammies that her sister had sent for Christmas the year before. He loved them, but they were way too small. She hadn't noticed till now. She thought, *We could cut the feet off them so they aren't stretched out like that,* and instantly felt overwhelmed by the thought, closing her eyes.

Anna didn't want to call Sam. She knew Sam had a busy week at work. She didn't usually work on Fridays, but she was today. And she didn't want Sam to see this side of her, this weakness.

"No, sweetie, we're okay, right? Just me and you? We'll be fine. Sam is working. I'm going to take a bath, and then I'll feel better. Will you be okay until I get out?"

He nodded uncertainly, took off his jammies to pee, then pulled them up and headed back out to the living room.

Anna ran the water and got in. *Not too hot,* she thought. *Careful.* If she passed out and hit her head, Phoenix would be all alone.

She got in and felt soothed by the water. She closed her eyes and almost fell asleep again, then jerked awake. She desperately wanted some green tea, to wake her up. In the white tile at the side of the bathtub the window behind her was reflected; the trees in the tile bent and shimmied, a greenish-yellow shadow movie. She watched it then slipped under the water to wash her hair.

When she got out she felt a little better. She got dressed and checked her phone. Sam wouldn't have called, because as far as she knew Anna was at work. The night before Anna had pretended everything was fine when Sam texted asking how they were doing. But Anna had a missed call, from an unknown 510 number.

"Anna, it's Ms. Martin calling. Sorry—Marie. I hope you're feeling better. Listen, I told my brother what happened yesterday, he's a doctor at Alta Bates, and he talked to his colleague, who's a neurologist. She's concerned about your symptoms and would like you to go in and see her

ASAP. She said she could even fit you in today or tomorrow. Please call her. I'll text you the number. And let me know if you need anything. This is my cell."

Anna sank to the floor and threw her phone across her bedroom. It bounced and slid under the bed. She sat there, shivering, her hair wet against her neck, then crawled under the bed to get it.

Claire would be home. She would help. "What's up, buddy?" Claire answered, and Anna started to cry. She shut her door so Phoenix wouldn't hear.

She'd missed Claire, Anna realized, the closeness they'd had.

"I'm sorry I've been AWOL," Anna told Claire. "I miss you."

"I miss you too. What's up? Are you at work?"

"No. I wasn't well enough to go, or even to take Phoenix this morning. He's home with me. I don't know what's happening. I'm not well. Yesterday I had a seizure at school and then a migraine, and today I vomited." She told Claire about the message from Marie Martin.

"You have to go, Anna. They're making it so easy for you. Go see what this is about."

"What about Phoenix?"

"I can come get him on my way to get Skyla. He can stay with us this weekend."

"The whole weekend?"

"Yeah, sure. We'll have fun. Skyla will be off her rocker with joy."

"Okay. So I go see the neurologist."

"Yeah. I wish I could go with you, but I'll have the kids. Could Sam go?"

"I don't want to tell her," Anna said.

"You haven't told her any of this??"

"No."

"Oh, Anna. Listen, have you eaten? I could bring you some stuff from Gregoire."

"Oh, I love you," Anna said. "Mmm, potato puffs. Thank you."

Anna called Sam that night and told her she was sick, that Claire had taken Phoenix for the weekend but Anna didn't want Sam to come over and get sick too. Especially since Sam had a big work weekend ahead.

"Can I bring you some soup? I could leave it on the stoop."

"No, thank you. I'm actually kind of nauseated. Stomach flu, I think."

"Oh, bunny… I want to hug you."

"I know, me too. But I'm a mess."

"I love you, Anna."

The offering she always made of it. The intentionality. It made Anna feel like she didn't say it good enough, like she didn't do it good enough. It pierced through her resolve to handle this on her own, like a flashlight in the fog, seeking her out, her inner self that was the part Sam wanted. Her heart.

"Get well soon. Call me if you need me."

And they hung up.

Anna didn't mention the seizure, the migraine, or the six-months-to-a-year death sentence she'd just received from the neurologist.

Part 2:
The Moon

Chapter 16

*T*he first night was a new moon. Nothing to see from the porch but uninterrupted darkness. The next night, there was just a sliver of a moon—so fine, like the hair of an elf. The following night, the moon was so bright on its thin underbelly that Anna almost felt she could see the other side, shining on all the places she'd never been.

She watched it every night. All of the moons, after all of the days. The full moons that were nature's perfect circle, more perfect than anything she could think of. She longed for them, saved up for them, earned them and put them in the bank. The days were short and the moon rose after Phoenix was asleep, so sometimes she had a joint with her moon. But it was the moon that was the medicine.

Her head felt like a full moon too, ready to pop.

She'd only told Marie Martin, at first. She figured Marie would find out anyway, and Anna needed her help. Twice she had felt about to pass out, and she knocked on the wall their classrooms shared; Marie quickly came to watch her class for her, or sent a parent. Anna had always hated having parents in her classroom, but Marie loved to put them to work, and Anna was grateful. She had promised Marie that she would tell the principal what was going on with her before Spring Break.

The weekend after her diagnosis, Anna had numbed herself with painkillers, baths, sleep, and horror movies. It seemed to her that if you let news like this sink in right away it would kill you on the spot. Telling people would only make it real.

By Sunday afternoon, she couldn't outrun the fear any longer. She called her sister.

Allie was the only place Anna could go. The only person Anna wasn't worried about worrying. Her sister owed her.

Anna told her everything: Glioblastoma. A star-shaped sucker that lived in her brain, stuck tight to the cells around it. Surgery was out because of the location of the tumor, and it was too late for chemo or radiation.

The neurologist hadn't skimped on the gory details about what Anna could expect to experience. Loss of brain function was the thing that spooked her most—the ability to make good decisions around Phoenix's care, when it would be essential to do so.

Anna had sensed a tinge of gloating in the woman, a subtle *I told you so*. Did she think this was Anna's fault?

Allie was quiet on the other end.

"I need you be strong," Anna said, hearing a sniffle.

"I'll be strong. Whatever you need."

"What I need is an adoption. I need Sam to be Phoenix's parent."

"Oh, Anna. You sure?"

"I'm sure," Anna said firmly. "Can you do that? If we come for Christmas?"

"Oh, the girls would love that," Allie said. "That would be so great. And yeah, I could put the papers together."

"That would be the best Christmas present you could give me."

"Have you talked to Sam about it already?"

"I will. Oh, and I need a will too."

"Okay."

"Thanks. That's a big relief. And it will be good to see you guys. I'll check with Sam—maybe we can come on Christmas Eve, stay a few nights."

She'd promised her sister that she would tell Sam.

The next day, Monday, Anna had sat in the sun on her lunch break and let it warm her face.

She felt a surprising new invincibility. Nothing could hurt worse than death; everything else was easy. The sun made her feel strong.

She knew she had to tell Sam. *Just a little more time in the sun,* she thought. *Just a little more honeymoon.*

Or maybe, Anna thought then, *it could all be honeymoon.* If she never told Sam, they could ride their honeymoon all the way out to the end. They could slip into the sunset, like that first day, after the ice cream, when she'd watched Sam skate away into the yellow and gray sky.

For now she would talk to Sam about Portland, and the adoption. They could fly together, in an airplane, the three of them, for the first time.

Anna closed her eyes and imagined flying with them, over Oakland, over the treetops, holding hands.

Anna's phone rang. The ring tone she'd chosen for Sam, "You're the One that I Want" from *Grease.*

"Whatcha doin'?" Sam asked when she picked up.

"Thinking of you."

"Me too, thinking of you. You should come get tattooed. I miss that ass."

"You can see my ass anytime you want."

"Are you feeling better?"

"Mm-hmm. Can I ask you a favor?"

"Anything."

"I have to go back in soon, but I was thinking…I would really love it if we were a real family. Like if you adopted Phoenix."

"Oh, wow."

"My sister's a lawyer, she does adoptions all the time. She offered, actually. She invited us to come to Portland for Christmas and she can do the paperwork while we're there."

"Wow. Okay. Yeah! I would love for Phoenix to be my son. Yes."

Anna shut her eyes after saying goodbye, fighting back tears of relief. It would be the three of them, flying together, for however long they had.

Transitions #6: Phases

Guess what, you guys? I'm adopting the boy. I'm going to be a papa! It's the name that feels right, and Anna says I get to choose.

I called my own dad "Dad," back when I called him anything. He has Alzheimer's now. Doesn't remember me, doesn't know how to put together the puzzle of me. Never really did.

We've established how hard it is even for evolving human brains to crack the non-binary code. When my dad's addled mind does remember me, he remembers a daughter (a tomboy, but still). But the me who actually shows up to visit is not that.

The last time I tried, it hurt too much, being rejected on every level. As if he was saying "no" to who I am, to what I was. That was a few years ago. I can only assume that the dementia has progressed much further by now.

I imagine it like a moon, moving across the sky of his mind, in all its phases. The darkness, the emptiness, covering over understanding, knowledge, language, memory. I imagine the erasure bringing a kind of peace, the way the night wipes out the memory of an unhappy day.

New moon, waxing crescent, first quarter, waxing gibbous, full moon, waning gibbous, third quarter, waning crescent.

No dementia seen, subjective memory loss, early-stage dementia, mild cognitive impairment, middle-stage dementia, moderate cognitive decline, late-stage dementia, severe cognitive decline.

And then the final stage, the end of the cycle: very severe cognitive decline.

I can think of nothing worse than forgetting everything you ever knew. And I hate that this is the first place my mind goes when I think about becoming a parent. The fear that someday this could happen to me.

Could happen to Anna.

Could happen to Phoenix.

If all the memories are gone, did they actually happen? If my dad—who, to be fair, wasn't really *my* dad even before he got Alzheimer's—is devoid of anything that would tie him to me, does that mean he is free of me, or that I am free of him?

I'll tell you the truth: I wish that were true. But while it may be that simple for him, it isn't for me. I still long for him to meet my child.

My resentment kicks in about all I've missed, starting a family late in life. Watching myself wander down to the road of feeling sorry for myself, alone, and instead turning back to them. Writing about it instead.

Thank you for listening. And for all of your support. <3

PHOENIX

I have two cousins named Violet and Dahlia. They are twins, 2 years old. That sounds like something out of a story but it's true.

They are much smaller, about half as big as me. And they are white, not brown, and there are two of them, not one.

They are a tiny army. When they are being bad, Mama says to Auntie Allie, just wait till they are 3.

But our trip to Portland was really fun. I got a dragon hand puppet for Christmas from Sam that looks so much like Saffron it is amazing! Saffron is yellow with red wings and this one is red with yellow wings. And of course Saffron is much smaller, she is tiny, she could never fit around my hand.

So the puppet is handy. Ha ha, handy! I like to make it say the things Saffron says, because then it's like everyone can see Saffron. I named the puppet Saffron too. Everyone thinks I'm hilarious but really it's Saffron. She says funny things and I just announce them. I can't think of an example at the moment but I will next time.

There was snow in Portland! We went in the hot tub and drank hot chocolate and the snow fell on us in the tub and in our hot chocolate! If you look closely at the water you could see a little fireworks when the snowflakes hit the water. I like to walk around under the water like a crocodile or a shark. Violet and Dahlia would shriek when I got near them. After a while Auntie Allie would call for their dad, "Leo, come and get the babies." Leo was mostly working but when he was there he was nice. He gave me a cookie that he made and it was lemon and warm and sugar-crunchy on top.

Also we took an airplane with Sam! Two airplanes! Also Sam is going to adopt me! So she will be my papa. I always was thinking about my dad, in India, I never thought I would meet a dad here.

The airplane from San Francisco to Portland took less than two hours. I thought it was far-er away, where my cousins live, since we don't go there very much, but it's close! In a plane everything is not very long away.

Chapter 17

*A*nna hadn't been back to the doctor. She would need to soon, to get her prescriptions refilled.

She hadn't told Sam. She couldn't risk losing her; she was going to need Sam to help her through this. To help with Phoenix.

All she could do was fight. Make it through each day, to get to the moon.

And then one day, as she headed to her email, a headline caught her eye:

Portland Activist Chooses Death with Dignity

Brittany Maynard wants to be the one to end her life—not the glioblastoma in her brain.

"After months of suffering from debilitating headaches," Maynard explained, "I learned that I had brain cancer. In an effort to stop the growth of my tumor, I had a partial craniotomy and a partial resection of my temporal lobe. Both surgeries were unsuccessful."

Maynard and her husband decided to move from San Francisco to Portland, Oregon, so she could access Oregon's Death with Dignity Act, which was passed in 1997. The law "allows terminally ill Oregonians to end their lives through the voluntary self-administration of lethal medications, expressly prescribed by a physician for that purpose."

Now, Maynard is on a mission to make people aware of the growing Death with Dignity movement, which empowers people with terminal illness to be able end their life on their own terms. To qualify, one must be both mentally competent and a resident of Oregon state, or one of the other four states where it's legal.

Maynard said that when doctors gave her a prognosis of six months to live, they prescribed full brain radiation. "The hair on my scalp would have been singed, my scalp covered with first-degree burns. My quality of life, as I knew it, would be gone.

"The recommended treatments would have destroyed the time I had left, and they would not have saved my life. Even with palliative medication, my pain could become constant. My personality would probably change completely and I might lose control of my verbal, cognitive, and motor functions."

Maynard discovered the aid in dying movement, an end-of-life option for terminally ill patients with a prognosis of six months or less to live. Though no one is pressured into using this option, and few people do, it provides an important choice for those who need it: a prescription from a physician for medication that they can self-ingest to end their dying process if it becomes unbearable.

Maynard knows that she might suffer in hospice care for weeks or even months. "My family would have to watch that. I didn't want them to have to suffer like that, so I decided death with dignity was the best option for us. I met the criteria, so I moved to Oregon to establish residency. I know that I am lucky, because most people don't have the resources to make these kinds of changes."

Brittany Maynard says that though she has had the medication for weeks, "I am not suicidal. I do not want to die. But I am dying. And I want to die on my own terms.

"Having the prescription filled and in my possession has given me a tremendous sense of relief. If I decide to change my mind about taking the medication, I will not take it, but having this choice at the end of my life has given me a sense of peace during a time when I would otherwise be overwhelmed by fear and uncertainty."

The medication, Maynard says, has given her a safety net, so that she can enjoy her final days. And she wants others to have the same option. "If you ever find yourself in my position, I hope you will have the same choice, to leave if your suffering becomes too great. To pass peacefully, with your loved ones around you."

Anna remembered that Allie had actually offered Anna their house in Portland for the summer, since she and her family would be in Europe. Anna had said no, not liking the idea of leaving home.

Now she remembered the hot tub in Allie's backyard, how you could see the moon from it.

She could watch the moon rise every night, and then at the end of the summer, if she was suffering, she could die with dignity, like Brittany Maynard.

I could do this on my own terms. She felt weak with relief at the thought of it, a release from the pain, from the fear.

The sun and the moon and hot water to ease her pain. If it got too bad to handle, she could float away….

She decided to tell her sister that yes, they would watch the house while Allie and Leo and the twins were in Europe. Maybe Sam could be a guest artist at her friend's tattoo shop in Portland.

Maybe Sam and Phoenix wouldn't even have to see her get sick. Maybe she wouldn't even have to tell them.

Part 3:
Portland

Chapter 18

*S*am and Phoenix loved Portland so much, it was easy to convince them to spend the summer there. They drove up the weekend after Anna and Phoenix finished school in June.

The house was a yellow Victorian in the Hawthorne district, with everything they needed in walking or biking distance. A friend of Allie's had lent them her daughter's old bike, for Phoenix, and Sam was tall enough to ride Leo's bike. Though Anna was embarrassed at first by the giant handlebars of her sister's cruiser bike, she grew to love cruising around, the three of them. It was like Mr. Rogers' neighborhood. There was a different farmers market in Portland every damn day.

And the house…she had always loved this house, and being in it just the three of them, without her sister and her nervous energy, or Leo, who always made her feel self-conscious, or her nieces, who were lovely but sucked all the air out of the room… Being in the house, just the three of them, was pure bliss.

There was a nice, quiet living room, a giant TV, with cable; a little family room off the entry that was a playroom for Dahlia and Violet. So much stuff.

The kitchen was smallish, as was the bathroom, but the bedroom, where she and Sam and sometimes Phoenix slept, was dark and cozy and Anna loved it.

Leo had converted the garage into a studio, and Allie's paintings were scattered about; Anna liked to sit at her sister's desk and look at her books, her things, for some clue about who Allie really was. She had never really understood her sister, and she wanted to.

Anna wrote Allie an email:

Hey sis, sitting at your desk, thinking of you. Hope you are eating all the cheese you can stand. We are taking care of things here. Everyone's so friendly! Thanks for giving us this chance to get away. It's so nice being here in your sweet yellow house.

Love to you four from us three—

Big A

Anna hadn't told her sister about the suicide pill. Or mentioned that she still hadn't told Sam about the tumor.

We decided to wait to tell Phoenix, I want to enjoy my time with him, Anna imagined telling her sister.

She would deal with all of that later. For now she wanted to focus on this new paradise, this surprising land of tropical flowers and incredible coffee.

Chapter 19

*B*efore long, though, Anna didn't know how much longer she could keep her illness from them. Being altogether under one roof meant less privacy. She had passed out in the bathroom and Sam had heard her fall and come running. Anna had convinced her she was okay, but she hated lying, and she was losing the strength to keep it up.

And then, one morning, an alert popped up on her phone.

Death with Dignity Advocate Brittany Maynard Dies at 29

Brittany Maynard has fulfilled her final wish. When the 29-year-old was diagnosed earlier this year with a fatal brain tumor, she was told the cancer would probably kill her within six months. But she had no intention of allowing the disease to control how she lived, or how she died.

Yesterday, Maynard ended her life on her own schedule, with the help of a doctor-prescribed lethal mixture of sedatives. The seizures and headaches that accompanied the final stages of her cancer had become too excruciating, and she chose to bring her suffering to an end by taking the aid-in-dying medication she had received months ago—a choice authorized under the

Oregon Death with Dignity Act.

"My glioblastoma is going to kill me, and that's out of my control," Maynard had shared on her website. "I've discussed with many experts how I would die from it, and it's awful. Being able to choose to go with dignity is less terrifying."

Advocates of the Death with Dignity Act staunchly oppose the notion that people who choose this option are committing suicide. "People choose this not because they are severely depressed," said a spokesperson, "but to maintain some aspect of control in their lives."

Maynard, who had fought in her final days to increase awareness about Death with Dignity, spoke about her frequent seizures, loss of balance, and terrifying moments of forgetting her husband's name. "I have a very large brain tumor, and it's killing me. I'm not killing myself. I don't want to die. People who commit suicide are typically people who want to die.

"I am choosing to go in a way that will mean less suffering and less pain. Not everybody has to agree that it's the right thing, because they don't have to do it. For me, it has provided a lot of relief, because the way that my brain cancer would take me is a horrible way to die."

An obituary was posted to her website, where friends have been posting farewells. "Brittany chose to make a well-thought-out and informed choice to die with dignity, in the face of a painful and incurable illness," the obituary reads. "She moved to Oregon to pass away in a place that strives to protect patient rights and autonomy, since her home state of California was not able to provide terminally ill patients with the same choice."

The obituary explained, "As Brittany's condition worsened and the tumor took over control, it became increasingly difficult for her to function. Her sole comfort was in being able to end her suffering before she was unable to function at all. We are comforted that she had this choice.

"She died as she intended—peacefully, in her bedroom, in the arms of her loved ones. In her final hours, she wanted to express her deep thanks to all of her wonderful friends and supporters."

Maynard's resolve was palpable: "I want people to be educated about this topic, to have discussions based on facts, not fear, and really have it be a healthcare choice, which is what makes it a freedom. I won't live to see the Death with Dignity movement reach critical mass, but I call on you to carry it forward. I have to believe that the pain we've endured has a greater purpose."

Anna stared at her phone, tears frozen in her eyes. Just then, Sam walked in. When she saw the look on Anna's face, she quickly looked at Anna's phone, to see what she was looking at. Anna went to swipe it away but she was too slow. Sam grabbed her hands and stilled them, then leaned over her, reading the article.

Anna read it with her, again. When Sam finished, she turned Anna's chair to face her and knelt before her, still holding her hands, as though Anna might run if she let go. She was silent, her eyes dark and expectant.

"It's why we're going to Portland," Anna said finally. "Death with dignity."

"For who?" Sam asked.

"For me." Anna's face heated up and the tears in her eyes melted and fell.

"What?"

"I have a brain tumor." Anna laughed, a high, hysterical, hyena-like sound. "I'm sorry. It's not funny."

"How can you have a brain tumor? What? For how long?"

"How long have I had it or how long will I have it for?"

"Anna! Will you tell me—what? What are you telling me?"

Sam's face fell apart. There were the tears Anna had been watching for all this time. But Sam's face when it was crying was terrible, a desert, lifeless.

Anna looked away, tried to pull her hands back. Sam held on, squeezed them harder.

"Let go," Anna said, and Sam released her.

"I'm sorry. But Anna, you can't just drop it there like a dead rat. What the fuck!"

"I've got a few months left to live, probably. Allie offered the house and I thought, you know, if I'm not better by the end of the summer, I'll do what she did, Brittany Maynard. Die with dignity…"

"No!" Sam pulled Anna off the chair and into her, on the floor. She clenched her fist as if she wanted to hit something, then pounded gently on Anna's back. "No," she said, shaking.

Anna felt frozen. She sat still, waited. Sam pulled back, let Anna go. She swatted at her tears. "How could you not tell me? Who knows?"

"My sister. And Marie at school. That's it. I didn't want you to worry. I was afraid you would make me go back to the doctor."

"I'm not going to make you do anything. It's your life."

"It's my death too. Okay? This is what I want. Will you let me? If it gets bad? It helps me feel less scared, of what might happen, how bad it might get."

"It makes sense now," Sam said. "The falling. The headaches. I'm sorry I didn't see it."

"I was hiding it from you. I'm glad you know now though, because I hated hiding it. I'm sorry I did…I just…I just didn't want you to see me differently."

Sam pulled her in again and held her tight, rocking back and forth and shaking her head. Her face was turned away from Anna.

How much did she need to say, to make Sam understand? "The pain is already so bad, and it's going to get worse. I'll probably start forgetting stuff. I don't want you and Phoenix to see me lose my mind. I want things to be good until the end. Can we do that?"

Anna held her breath, afraid Sam would say no.

Minutes passed. Sam's body was vibrating with tears.

Finally Sam calmed herself, took a deep breath. "You can have whatever you want."

Her voice was emotionless, and Anna knew it must have been hard for Sam to give her this. She let out the big breath she'd been holding in and squeezed Sam with all her strength. "Thank you."

"Phoenix?" Sam asked quietly. "Do we tell Phoenix?"

"I don't think so. We'll spend the sweetest, best time with him this summer, it'll be all goodness and light. He's old enough, he'll remember me for the rest of his life. And he has you now. Are you up to being his parent on your own?"

Sam nodded into her shoulder. "Yes." She turned her head into the space between Anna's head and her shoulder, her nose to Anna's neck, breathing her in.

"You smell like fire," she said.

Chapter 20

*F*or every bad day, there was a good day. Some bad days had good in them, and the good ones had shitty moments too, of course. Anna decided that when the ratio became more weighted toward bad, that would be how she'd know it was time to stop.

If 1 was a good day, and 2 was a bad day, the previous two weeks had looked like: 1, 2, 1, 2, 2, 2, 1111, 1222.

Anna had become obsessed with numbers ever since she started watching the moon. She counted everything and obsessed over symmetries. It all had to make some kind of sense, and math seemed more likely than words. Numbers calmed her, for the first time in her life. She found herself strangely quiet.

She didn't want to think about leaving Phoenix, so she didn't. She recalled the equation from their pizza-making, $2 + 1 = 3 - 1 = 2$. The balance of before and after was a simple comfort.

She focused everything she had on Phoenix. She looked at him and looked at him, enough looks to last her forever. "Mom!" he finally said when she'd stared at him for too long. He had started calling her Mom since they arrived in Portland, probably because he was afraid the kids down the block would think he was a baby if he said "Mama." Anna at first thought it was a bit early to be "Mom" and mourned the loss of "Mama." Then she realized it was an opportunity, to hear him address her how he would have when he got older. She imagined a tween Phoenix, a Phoenix taller than her, then taller than Sam.

Phoenix Ravi Harvey Stray. She would have to tell his dad, that she was leaving. That was how she had been thinking of it: leaving. She imagined herself flying away, carried away by a phoenix, fire-tailed and rainbow-scaled. They would fly away together.

Her Phoenix would be staying here.

He would be with Sam. Sam would be good, a mom and dad both. She'd been taking Phoenix skating, on Anna's bad days. Or to work at the tattoo parlor, or to a park. Portland spent the summer in a perpetual state of celebration.

Anna was glad for the sun but found she needed the shadows more. For the first time in his life she didn't have to be okay, for the boy. She took the space Sam gave her, and dove into it, raging.

The basement of the house had concrete walls and floors, a musty smell. She went down there and screamed, smashing her fists against the washing machine. She pulled down the white cotton sheets Allie had left hanging and tangled herself up in them on the cold concrete floor, curled into a ball inside a fitted one. She screamed into it, punched it, loving and hating the feeling of being contained, growling and feeling like the animal that she was, that she had always been.

She threw her phone against the concrete wall with all of her strength, then left it where it landed, not wanting to have anything to do with it or the outside world. A few days later she found it charging next to her bed. Sam had found it and brought it up, and though the screen was shattered, despite Anna's best efforts it still worked. It would be Anna's last phone.

She thought about what it would feel like. When she left. Would it hurt? Would she feel herself leaving and want to come back? She was terrified to say goodbye to Phoenix, and to Sam. She hadn't thought about what a terrible responsibility it would be, so many decisions that would be hers to make.

How could she possibly purposely leave her son behind? How could she ever have thought that choosing to leave him would be easier than being taken from him naturally?

This was a purely selfish decision, this "death with dignity." She felt now that she'd chosen it rashly. It was simply there to make her less scared.

Yet how could she stay? She was turning into an old woman before their eyes: brittle bones, graying hair, in constant pain.

She took pills—for the pain, and also for the anger. Before they left Oakland the neurologist had prescribed an anticonvulsant, and steroids. The Oxy made things a bit bearable, lighter. Like living in a cloud. Or a fitted sheet.

Transitions #7: PDX

Burnside in the house! Yo, this shit is ON! If you haven't been to the Burnside Skate Park, seriously, check it out.

I took the boy yesterday. I'm teaching him to skate. I perched him at the top of a bowl that no one skates up, and I skated around and around the bowl, showed him how.

We've been practicing, in parking lots and parks. Wherever, anywhere. The infinite playground of a new urban environment, a whole adventure of possibility. So many things to climb and flip around, to run up and jump off of. He wears shoulder and knee pads and a helmet, and I gave him my first board, the one I learned on. It seems like a good time to teach him, while he's still pretty fearless.

I wish I could remember how that felt. I fight with fear all the time now. That Phoenix will hurt himself. That I will.

All my injuries. The ACL alone…I would never want for Phee to experience that pain.

But I toss my fears up in the air, smash them with my invisible light saber, then sink into the bowl. The adrenaline is an antidote, it's more powerful than the fear. I fight the fear with fun. More, more, more fun.

Burnside is complicated, with its switch-ups and mysteries lying on the other side. And, I'm getting older. I fuckin' hate to admit it, but I'm slowing down. I mean, I do have a 5-year-old with me, so I can't go too crazy, but anyway it's not really an urge in me anymore. I enjoy riding each bowl how it was designed to be ridden. There are some hella good skaters here, and Phoenix and I like to sit and watch them. Enjoy the graf.

It's a whole other world, with this kid in it. It has depth and shape, is clean and clear. No mysteries on the other side.

How did I end up with this incredible human being who gets me like no one else has ever gotten me? I swear. I love him from such a fierce, humble place in myself, a place I never knew was there.

Chapter 21

Anna and Sam decided they needed a night out. They'd never gone dancing together. Allie's baby-sitter was happy to watch Phoenix.

They went to a queer night at a club that Sam had heard was cool; she'd tattooed the DJ the week before. When they got there they found her at the DJ booth, and Sam checked on her tattoo, a wolf on her right shoulder, to see how it was healing.

Anna felt a little shy at first, a little fragile out in the world, but after a few mojitos from the Slurpee machine on the bar she was feeling fine. The whole night felt slushy, Anna's body falling in with Sam's, with the others'. From the bar to the dance floor and back to the bar, to the photo booth, to the dance floor, the bar. An art student had set up a little portrait studio in one of the club's back rooms, and they sat and kissed while they had their portrait drawn.

Then they went next door to the bathroom, and Sam got Anna in a stall and shut the door, and then pulled out what she was packing and fucked Anna, gently, against the bathroom door.

They were both a bit drunk though and while they had a great time, kissing wildly, neither one of them could come. Eventually they gave up and went out and danced some more.

Anna didn't even have to think about it; her body moved with Sam's like something dependent in nature, cause and effect. She let the music take her over, shook it all around, hooking her hands in Sam's belt, matching Sam's hips as they ground deeper into hers.

Prince came on, "Let's Go Crazy," and they did. They sang the words to each other:

"Electric word, life, it means forever, but I'm here to tell you: there's something else," Sam lip-synched to Anna. "The afterlife."

"A world of never-ending happiness," Anna lip-synched, dramatically, back. "You can always see the sun—day and night."

They jumped up and down, Anna put her hands up above her and danced around like a pogo stick. Then she put her hands on her hips and swerved from side to side, singing "What's it all for?" as Sam pulled Anna's hips to hers.

They took a taxi home, and by the time they got there Anna had to pee so bad they decided to just go outside. Looking up from their squats, they saw the baby-sitter peering out at them, over their heads. Whispering now, they peed together in Anna's front yard, holding hands, in the dark.

Chapter 22

*I*n the backyard, there was a pond with turtles and koi, a little waterfall that flowed over some rocks, and a tree with purple flowers that the hummingbirds liked. In the middle of the pond was a plant with curly tendrils that boinged out into the world.

Anna watched the world from the hot tub, the girls' mini ocean animals lined up on the rim, feeling like she was in a terrarium, a complete world unto itself, becoming ever more real. She started going in the tub morning, noon, and night, and the boundary between water and dry land grew as nebulous as the one between real life and dream life.

The plants blocked all the neighbors, so they could be naked back there. They had stopped adding chlorine, because Anna hated the smell. It smelled like cancer. Anna wondered if the tumor was made up of all the chemicals she had ingested in her life; maybe they had all gathered there over the years, binding together, joining forces. Sometimes she thought she could feel it growing.

She had grown skinny; she wasn't interested in food anymore. With Phoenix in her belly all she had wanted was mashed potatoes. Now all she could eat was hard-boiled eggs. They'd met a family with backyard chickens at the park; they had a daughter near Phoenix's age, and ever since Anna had mentioned her hard-boiled egg fixation the woman had brought over a few eggs every day. She placed them in their shoes on the porch first thing in the morning, just after they'd been laid. When Phoenix woke up in the morning, the first thing he did was check their shoes for eggs. Sometimes they were still warm.

Anna felt weird at first, about this kindness. It made her suspicious. Did they know, somehow, about her? But she was just being paranoid—how could anyone know? All these people had just met her. Her sister would never have told anyone, and neither would Sam. But still, everywhere they went—to the park, the grocery store, the food trucks and libraries and coffee shops—everyone was so damn nice.

"They're trying to get you to stay," Sam's friend at the tattoo shop told Anna when she brought it up. "It took me a while to get used to too. Things change in the winter; people become more internal. It's like everyone turns into extroverts in the summer, during our little window of sun. Portland's a big party suddenly. Even the depressives are happy."

Anna felt self-conscious about her skinny body, her breasts and hips disappearing, even though Sam told her she was beautiful every day. Sam said it was a shame about Anna's appetite, since Portland was such a good town for vegetarians. She had gained the weight that Anna had lost.

"And now that it's on, it's not going anywhere," Sam told them. "When I was young, the pounds came and went, but now that I'm old, they're on for good."

"You look good," Anna told her. "Right, Phoenix?"

Phoenix had gained some weight too, she noticed. He would be six soon. She was supposed to have been his teacher next year. The thought of teaching made her feel like her body was filled with quicksand.

"Don't say it, Phoenix, I know what you're thinking, you're thinking I'm fat!" Sam said.

"You're not fat," he said. "I'm fat!" He stood on the side of the hot tub and pushed his belly out, then jumped in, splashing them.

"Phoe-nix!" Anna said, and Sam laughed.

"Come here, you guys," Sam said, and they went to her. She held them to her so they didn't float away. They were quiet as they watched the birds play in the pond.

Anna watched the skies go by in the water of the hot tub. The sunlight, the clouds, the sunset, the moon. The ocean animals passed the days with her. They were always in a different place than they'd been when she'd seen them last, and she imagined that when they were alone they came alive. The whale shark and the dolphin, the seahorse and sea dragon and sea stars. The sea turtle, octopus, angelfish, sea lion.

She was 31 years old. She had expected to live three times this many years. It was impossible to understand.

Anna sunk her head under the water and looked up at the blank sky, letting her body float. Another thing that reminded her of pregnancy: how good the water felt. How easy it made letting go.

How good it would feel to let go.

But she wasn't ready yet. She brought her head out of the water and stretched her body behind her, looking back over her shoulder.

I'll burn so bright they'll never forget me.

PHOENIX

We went camping for my birthday. I'm 6 now!

We went out of Portland to a river called the Deschutes, which everyone says "da-chute." In the river we floated down it! Sam showed us how, she did floating at another river in Russia.

What you do is you hold on to the big circle, our three were green and called River Rats, and you just put your bum in the middle part and your legs off the side, and you just hold on! We did a thing where we all three held on to each other like a train. We also discovered a part where the river went really fast, and you have to steer to the deep part so you don't hit the rocks. It is fun but a little scary, you go really fast! Mama and Sam helped me but I learned it so by the time we left I was doing it all by myself, and even when they floated away from me I wasn't scared.

When you get to the end part, the water keeps going, but there are rocks where we got out. We did this all day— float down, climb out, walk back, float down, and again. Sometimes just me and Sam would go and Mama would watch. The sun was hot but we all had hats. Mama didn't want to put any sunscreen on and she got really red on the shoulders but she didn't care.

When the sun was going down we had one last float down the river, and then we got out and went back to our campsite. We got warmed up in our tent and had a tickle tournament, and then we went out and Sam made a fire. I helped, while Mama made dinner. Mac and cheese, the bunny one, and chik patties that we cooked on the fire, and corn too. When it was done Mama pulled back the husk and a cloud of smoke came out like a dragon breathing.

That reminded me, where is Saffron? I didn't see her all the time we were camping. Maybe she doesn't like camping?

For my birthday Mama made me a cake that was chocolate and raspberries and a number 6 candle that I blowed out and made a wish that I better not tell you or it might not come true.

And after that there was fireworks! On the river! Some people were out on a boat and they set them off. Sam said, "Oh yeah, I forgot to tell you that I ordered fireworks for Phoenix's birthday" and then she winked so that means she didn't really. But I loved them! All of the camping people stood in the water and watched them together and I played with some other kids that were there. We climbed up a tree and jumped down out of it into the water.

I like it here in Portland. I wish we could move here because then no George! But Mama says it doesn't work like that. Wherever you go, George follows you. He didn't follow me here though! She says that's because we're on vacation, which is not like real life, no bullies allowed.

Chapter 23

*S*am kept wanting to talk, but Anna didn't.

"It doesn't make me feel better," Anna said.

"But you said you want to do this in a healthy way, to be ready, right? That's how you get ready."

"That's how *you* get ready...."

"Well, can I at least ask you some questions? Are you going to give notice at work? If so, where should Phoenix go to school?"

"Peralta? I don't know. Anywhere."

"I think it would be easier for him somewhere else if you're not there."

"Maybe you're right. Peralta is a good school, but George is there. And I won't be there to keep an eye on him."

"Can we look at schools together, online?"

"Yes. Let's do that. He needs a good art program and teachers who appreciate him." Anna smiled, relaxing a little. "And yes, I am giving my notice. Fuck that place."

They laughed, and Anna realized it was a huge relief to have Sam be thinking about these things, so she didn't have to. She couldn't believe it hadn't even occurred to her to take Phoenix out of Peralta. She felt lighter at the thought. He could go anywhere. *We'll choose a new school for him. Together.*

Maybe she would even be able to go back with them,

to be with him as he started first grade.

The pain was pretty bad most days. The doctor had refilled her Oxy prescription and she tried not to worry about taking them, even though she knew they made her spacey.

It was hard for her to think about anything outside the house. She was lucky to have Sam steering their little yellow ship.

"Will you do a tattoo for me?" Anna asked Sam.

"Anytime."

"Tomorrow."

"Yes. Where?"

"Hmm. Shoulder maybe?" She pointed back at her left one, and then reached over to grab the other one. "Shoulders?"

"Beautiful. I can't wait."

Transitions #8: My New Drug

Do you guys know about the coffee in Portland? It is just mad good. People are so serious about it because it's so good. Or it's good because they're serious about it.

In the old days I would be at the bar right now, writing this, not the coffee shop. Beer went well with skating. And tattooing.

But up here, I bring a coffee into work. I haven't even thought about beer in days. Though they have great beer up here too.

Portland's a kind of utopia, the dangerous kind: it sucks you in in the summer and then sucks you dry over the winter. I've seen it happen. Friends from the Bay Area move to Portland, because SF is the most expensive place to live in the entire country—worse than Manhattan! Fuck this place, they say, and then a few months later you see them bitching about the Portland weather on Facebook. Then you don't hear from them for a while, and then, in a year or two, they're back, living in yet another share, soaking up the sun at Dolores Park.

Portland has these very wholesome attractions in the summer: movies and music in the park, floating down the river. They do this big float down the Willamette River, hundreds of people in the water together, right next to downtown Portland. Sounds kind of idyllic, right?

Anyway, I'm enjoying PDX, and the awesome fucking skate parks here especially, but all at an arm's length, because I don't want to get stuck here.

Oh, and I tattooed my girl again: *S* on one shoulder (that's me) and *P* on the other, for Phoenix. Beautiful black wings on her delicate white shoulder blades.

Chapter 24

One day Joey called from the Albany tattoo shop. Sam was driving. She turned the music down.

"I miss you, man," she said, on speaker.

"I miss you too. We're driving to Voodoo Doughnuts."

"Aw, I wish I was with you!"

"Us too," Sam said, smiling.

"Hi Joey!" Anna called.

"Hi Joey!" Phoenix chimed in from the back.

"Aw, man. You guys are so cute. Hi!"

"How are things?" Sam asked.

"Good. Business is slow since you're not here! And actually, I'm calling with news. I'm opening another shop, in SF. I finally found a space, in the Castro. Piercing and tattoos."

"Buddy, that's awesome!"

"I know. This great space opened up and I decided to grab it. I was hoping you might consider working for me there, instead of Albany. Manage it, maybe."

"Woah. That is a sweet offer. When are we talking?"

"In the next few months. Fall, probably."

"Okay. I'm gonna have to think about it. Thanks for asking. Let's talk soon."

"Okay, man. Talk to you soon. Hey, you guys, eat a doughnut for me! Or two, or three!" She laughed and they said bye and hung up.

Sam's eyes were lit up like diamonds, Anna could see even from the passenger seat. She turned the music back up, lost in thought.

When Sam looked over at Anna, she had a question in her face. "Could I do that? Could Phoenix go to school in SF?" Sam asked quietly.

"Maybe, yeah. Lots of good elementary schools there."

"Let's look at schools when we get home. We could look at private schools too. One of my friends, her son is on full scholarship. If they want your kid, sometimes you can get a good deal, I've heard."

Anna smiled. "There's a Waldorf school in the Mission. That would be amazing for Phoenix."

"Okay. So we'll look when we get home. And you're okay that I consider this?"

"Yes. Maybe I'll come."

Sam went quiet.

"If I don't stay here."

The guy standing in front of them in line at Voodoo Doughnuts was talking loudly about physician-assisted suicide.

"I don't know why they allow all those people to come up here just to kill themselves. It's, like, a selling point to this city. It's kind of gross."

His friend answered, more quietly, and they guy responded, "Yeah, but it's not natural!"

Sam tapped him on the shoulder and asked him to lower his voice.

"Why?" he asked.

"You're talking kind of loudly."

The guy shook his head at her and turned back around to face the front, pretending to peruse the long list of doughnuts on the front wall.

Anna felt humiliated, like it was obvious to everyone in the line why Sam had made a fuss. She, Anna, was one of *those people.* She had moved here just to kill herself, and once her new ID came in the mail from the DMV, she could go to a doctor and get one of *those pills.*

She felt her cheeks grow hot. She knew she should be grateful to Sam for shutting the guy up, but all she felt was embarrassed and very tired.

Sam picked Phoenix up and put him on her shoulders so he could see the board.

"Voodoo Doll," he said. "Peach Fr-it-ter. Dirt?"

Anna looked up at Phoenix, and then quickly to Sam. Their eyes all registered the same surprise.

"I can read them," Phoenix said. "I can read!"

Chapter 25

*T*hey went to see *The Pink Panther* at Pix, an arty pastry shop that served wine and cocktails and showed movies on their back patio in summer. Sam and Anna both adored Peter Sellers and were excited to introduce Phoenix to him.

The pastries were whole worlds in miniature—Willy Wonka on acid. Sam and Anna ordered champagne, and Phoenix chose from the menu, reading it himself and ordering the craziest chocolate masterpiece on the menu: the Shazam.

When it came—caramel mousse and chocolate cake, surrounded by a dense and elaborate chocolate wall—Phoenix broke into it with a mania. Just as the movie came on.

By the time Peter Sellers slipped off the globe and onto the floor, Anna had a bad feeling in her stomach. By the time he set off fireworks in the middle of the party, she was barfing up her champagne.

The smell was terrible, but everyone tried not to react, being polite Portlanders. Still, Anna heard someone say "Ew" under their breath. But the patio was so full of people, Anna couldn't get out of there in time to make it to the bathroom. It kept coming, so all she could do was try to aim for the plate in the middle of the table. Phoenix had grabbed his Shazam off the table and was holding it aloft, near his chest.

Sam had her arm around Anna's back and her hand on Anna's chest. Anna looked around in desperation. Some people were watching her, to see what would happen; others were looking around for the waiter, who was suddenly, conspicuously missing; the rest were watching the movie, not knowing what else to do. Anna smiled at Phoenix, who looked worried, to let him know it was okay.

"You tell me when you're ready to go," Sam said.

"Now," Anna said.

"Let's go, dude," Sam said and Phoenix hopped off his chair, taking his pastry and holding it delicately in his palm, leaving the plate on the table.

The other customers watched them go. The waiter had finally showed up and was asking if they were okay.

"I made a mess," Anna told him. Sam had handed her a handkerchief to wipe her face, but she had little chunks of vomit on her sweater, and in her hair.

"That's quite alright," the waiter said, and Sam gave him some cash for the bill as they headed out.

"We'll get the *Pink Panther* movies for you to watch at home," Sam told Phoenix.

"Yeah," Anna agreed weakly. They got to the Prius and Sam helped Anna into the front seat, then let Phoenix into the back. She held his pastry for him as he buckled his seatbelt gingerly, trying not to get chocolate everywhere.

"Is it okay if he eats this whole thing?" Sam asked. Most of the chocolate wall had been demolished but the whole base still stood.

Anna nodded. "Hopefully he doesn't start vomiting too." She laughed, and then looked over at Sam as she slid into the driver's seat. "No more champagne for me."

When Anna finally got around to researching her options, she was overwhelmed by the thought of all the doctor's appointments—by the thought of even trying to find a doctor.

"Sam?" she called.

Sam came into the studio and Anna asked, "Can you help me find a doctor? I don't care who it is, as long as they're nice."

"Of course," Sam said.

"And will you go with me? I got my ID in the mail today, so we can go anytime."

"Sure." Sam paused. "Wait, your ID? Oh." Anna could see her putting together that Anna didn't want to go to just any doctor—she wanted to find an assisted-suicide doctor.

"Thanks."

They met the doctor the following Thursday. Phoenix had a playdate with his friend from the park, the one with the chickens. Anna didn't know how, but she still had a sense that the kid's mom knew somehow, about her. The eggs, the offers of help…she was grateful, but she found it difficult to trust the other woman's motives. Not that it mattered—Phoenix was having fun, frolicking with backyard chickens, eating gourmet ice cream.

The doctor had long gray hair and a big silver beard; he had style, Anna could tell, even though he just wore a white coat over a sweater vest. She liked him. He seemed intrigued by her, by them, and like he actually cared what happened to her.

He explained the whole process to them, and answered their questions. No, it wouldn't hurt—the actual dying part. Yes, she could take the pill "to go" (she would pick it up from a pharmacy and then take it whenever she was ready). Anna knew that meant she could take the pill and go anywhere she wanted. What was to stop her from taking it back to the Bay Area?

The doc wanted to know about Anna's next-of-kin. Anna had come ready for this—she pulled out her will, and the adoption paperwork.

"Sam is my next-of-kin," she said.

"Are your parents alive?" he asked.

"They are, but I don't want to tell them."

"Are you sure?"

"I'm sure."

"Okay, well, that's your prerogative. I want you to think about it a little more, and we'll talk again next time I see you. In a little over two weeks. Okay? Looking at your X-rays, I think it's good you're starting this process now. These things can progress quickly after a certain point. Have you told your son that you're sick?"

"No," Anna said, shaking her head.

"Why not?" he asked kindly.

"He only just turned six," Sam said.

"Six is old enough to understand," he said. "Think if you were in his shoes. If you don't tell him, and he finds out that you knew, he would have every right to be angry, to not have been given the time for goodbyes that you had."

"I'll think about it." Anna looked at Sam. "We'll talk about it."

"Good. Call me if you have any questions or if you need anything at all."

Transitions #9: Death with Dignity

I have something to come clean about. I've been keeping it from you guys because I had to but now I don't have to anymore.

Anna, my beloved, has a brain tumor and only a few months to live. We moved to Portland so that she can do death with dignity, which is legal here. So she can have some control over the end. Like Brittany Maynard. That's where Anna got the idea.

We don't have a date, but we saw the doctor yesterday, and he says he supports Anna's decision, given her prognosis. There's still a process we have to go through, so it's not happening anytime soon. Right now we are waiting and seeing.

In the meantime, I wanted to reach out to anyone who has been through cancer or other terminal illnesses, or helped others through it. We are way too isolated with this shit, we need help. I need to figure out how to support Anna and Phoenix through this.

And then, you guys, I will be Phoenix's only parent, when she's gone. I am going to need support with that too.

PHOENIX

I found the Saffron puppet—she was under the bed. I saw a little of her yellow scales peeking out from under the bed and pulled her out and she was so, so mad that I had forgotten her under there. I put her on my hand and moved her mouth as I spoke for her. "Were you just gonna let me die under there?"

"No!" I told him. "I've been looking for you." But I kind of liked it better when she was away. She is mean sometimes.

I held her mouth closed. Then I pulled a shoelace around her mouth and tied it shut. I did a double knot like Sam taught me. So now she can't talk, or breathe any fire. She is my responsibility, so I have to be in charge of her and stop that happening.

My mom told me yesterday that she is very sick, so I have to be a big boy. That means managing my dragon. And not bothering her when it's something I can do myself, like make a PBJ. I know how to do that all by myself, so when I'm hungry I can just do it instead of bother Mama about it. Also Sam and Mama would like to have some time together. They didn't say that, but I know it's true.

Mama will probably not be able to even be my first-grade teacher. And I am probably not going back to Peralta school. Which is actually good news, because I won't have to see George anymore. Also we might move to San Francisco. That part is exciting.

Mama said we have to use the time we have together to be happy. So I tried so hard to be happy, to be smiling and not crying when they told me. We held hands at the kitchen table, Sam and me and my mama's.

This is why Mama had been so strange lately, looking at me so serious like she's trying to understand my face. And sleeping all the time. And falling down. And throwing up.

It's too scary to think about Mama not being here. So I'm not going to.

Chapter 26

*W*hen Anna woke up from her nap and found them gone, she panicked. Ever since they'd told Phoenix about the tumor, Anna had felt extra protective of him. It was like all that time she'd been keeping it from him she'd been keeping it from herself too, pretending it would be okay somehow. Telling him made it real. Which meant she really was leaving her son behind. Which was impossible.

And since Sam had blogged about it, her readers—both friends and strangers—had been offering their support too. Her blog post disclosing that they were moving to Portland so Anna could die with dignity now had 117 comments, far more than she'd received on any of her other posts. The site was getting traffic from people who wouldn't normally have read her blog, and they were all in support of Anna's decision.

Anna looked at the comments a few times a day, to see what new things people had written. It was a little scary, having her life (and death) be so out in the open like that—even though so far everyone had been positive and supportive. When Sam had asked her if it would be okay to talk about it, Anna had said yes without thinking, because it was good publicity for the cause. She knew there were terminally ill people out there who didn't know physician-assisted suicide was even a thing, and they might be suffering and scared. It was the only upside to having a terminal illness, as far as Anna was concerned. She would have control over when, and how, the end came. This thing that people fought against their whole lives, the not-knowing, Anna no longer had to be afraid of.

As long as she didn't wait too long. If she waited until she was too sick, then death could come for her before she was ready, or the worsening symptoms could keep her from having options, mobility, a clear mind. She wanted to be able to make good decisions, to not change too much from the partner and parent that Sam and Phoenix knew.

Her dreams were becoming more and more real. The things that happened there—when Anna woke, it was hard for her to comprehend that they hadn't really happened. And the things she thought about in her waking life, the places her brain went—they started to feel like they couldn't possibly be real, they must be a dream.

All alone in the quiet, in the darkening house.

She pushed herself out of bed. It was a good bed, Allie's bed, and Anna was glad, since she had been spending a lot of time in it. No wonder her waking and sleeping lives were starting to merge.

In the kitchen, she found a note from Phoenix. Ever since he realized he could read, his writing too had blossomed. She thought all of it had probably been advanced by his computer journal. Now that he was ready for it, reading and writing seemed to be just happening—organically, with no effort.

Mama,

We went to skate Burnside.

We love you,

Phoenix and Sam

Next to it, Sam had drawn a Sharpie drawing of the two of them skating. *He wrote the note and she illustrated it,* Anna thought.

It didn't feel safe, them being out after dark, away from her. Sam had left her phone behind, so Anna couldn't check in with them.

She French-pressed a cup of coffee and sat at the computer to drink it. She pulled open the file she was working on and tinkered with it. *How can I possibly finish it in time?*

She couldn't focus on it, though, worrying about them. For a while, the alone time had felt luxurious. She'd been happy to have extra time for her projects, especially this one. But lately she cared more about keeping Sam and Phoenix close.

Anna grabbed her bag and walked over to a bus stop on Hawthorne that she knew would take her to the Burnside Bridge. She'd never been to the skate park there but knew it was under the bridge. The Prius was parked nearby, but with the spotty vision the tumor had caused, it was safer to take the bus.

It came quickly and she got on, sat by a window, watched Portland go by. It was her first time taking a bus in Portland; it was clean, compared with Oakland buses.

I might not see Oakland again, she thought, and the sting of that was surprisingly sharp and deep. Oakland had become home, and she realized that the distrust she'd been feeling around Portland's persistent niceness was really homesickness.

She got off at the bridge and walked under it, into the darkness, her eyes searching out the skate park. She heard the crashing of wheels and looked in their direction, feeling the *S* and *P* on her shoulders, still sore, like divining rods leading her to them. *Right, left, right, left.* She let her shoulders lead the way, aware that she must look like John Wayne but not caring.

And then she saw them: Phoenix at the top of a big bowl, and then Sam swooping up and out of it, catching her board in her hands, then falling into it again, out of sight.

Anna felt the same thrill she'd felt when she first saw Sam skating at the Berkeley skate park: an excitement centered in her groin. There was also, now, a fear in her belly, that Sam would hurt herself. And, as she stared over at her, locating her lover in the lulls and lips, a new pain bloomed in her heart.

She was losing this amazing person. Her person. This star. Anna had finally found her and now she was going to lose her.

She stood watching them. No one saw her. Without her red lipstick she was invisible. She could walk through the world with the anonymity she had been wanting her whole life.

The quiet and clarity of this life of dying. The body broke down and the mind blurred but the heart became strong and clear. Everything was so much simpler. She understood how the world worked, how everything was not about her. She'd reached this blessed clarity decades ahead of schedule. Aging, evolving—all of her processes were sped up now.

She grew tired and sat on the concrete, watching the skaters fly and crash around her, more graceful than ballerinas. Their fluidity, the up and down, a dance with the concrete, with the board, with one another. Unchoreographed, a surprise every time.

She remembered skating from Olivia's house to Huntington Beach. Holding hands with Sam as they skated to the ocean. They'd only done it that one time. That was before she'd known about the tumor, and she recalled now how scared she had been, of hurting herself. She couldn't hurt herself, as Phoenix's only parent.

But she wasn't Phoenix's only parent anymore. And now that she was leaving, she realized, there was nothing she couldn't do. She could bungee-jump, zip-line, skydive, ride roller coasters without worrying about brain damage. Her brain was already damaged.

It wasn't her job to worry about all of this anymore. It was her job to do every scary thing she could between now and the end—and that meant telling Sam and Phoenix exactly how she felt, telling her sister how she felt too. That meant writing for real, and confronting every other scary thing she'd avoided.

She headed over to the bowl where Sam and Phoenix were, and as she rounded a corner she heard Sam's voice carry out: "Anna! Duck!" She went quickly to her knees and looked up just as a skateboard and its rider flew over her and then landed solidly in the next pool, looking back at her and grinning. She gave him a weak thumbs-up and said to herself, "That's what I'm talking about," as Sam skated up out of the bowl in front of her and jumped off her board, catching it and hugging Anna at the same time, saying, "That was awesome."

Phoenix waved wildly at her over Sam's shoulder. He looked so much bigger than she remembered.

Chapter 27

*A*nna's sister called from Paris, upset because she had heard from a friend about Anna's decision; the friend had seen Sam's blog post and sent it to Allie.

Allie was pissed, couldn't believe Anna hadn't told her.

"I haven't decided anything yet. There's no plan," Anna responded. "I would have gotten in touch before I did anything."

"I want to say goodbye to you!" Allie cried. "It's not fair to just leave without saying goodbye."

Anna fought her desire to hang up the phone. *This isn't about you,* Anna thought.

But then she thought, *Maybe it is. Maybe that's exactly what this is about. They are the ones being left behind.*

"When are you coming back?" Anna asked.

"End of August," Allie said. "I think it's the 27th."

"I promise I'll wait till then, okay? If I get super sick between now and then I'll call you, and maybe you guys can come back early. But I'll try to wait. I think I'll be okay until then."

"What about Mom and Dad?" Allie asked.

"What about them?" Anna snapped.

"Are you going to tell them?"

"That would mean talking to them," Anna said. That would mean talking to *her,* was really what she meant;

she didn't care so much about her dad. For a long time she'd been angry at him, like she had been at Allie, for letting her mom hurt her, but now she noticed she mostly felt ambivalent. He had left her mom finally when Anna moved out and quickly started a new family, but neither she nor Allie had ever met them. He had called on birthdays for a while but in recent years had stopped even doing that. Anna didn't even have a number for him, but she knew her sister did.

"Can I tell them?"

"Why? I don't want to see them. That's what she'd want. She'd make it into some big drama. I am so not up for that."

"Alright, well, if you change your mind, I'll call them for you." Allie paused, and then said, "She loves you, you know."

"She has a funny way of showing it."

"I know."

"Do you?" The words popped out of Anna's mouth.

"I do know. And I'm sorry."

"About what?" Anna needed to hear it.

"That I never did anything about it."

"Why didn't you?" Anna's voice softened. She couldn't believe it: they were finally telling the truth. They'd only ever talked around it, and she'd never known how much her sister knew. Allie was a few years younger, and the abuse had never happened right in front of her.

"I don't know. I was scared of her."

"But there was no one to protect me. Dad wasn't around, and you were always hiding in your room. She took it all out on me."

"I know, sweetie."

"Why didn't you ever say anything to me about this?"

"Because I'm a loser! I thought if you knew I knew,

you'd hate me even more than you already do."

"I don't hate you," Anna said quietly.

"I wouldn't blame you if you did."

"I don't want to hate you. I don't want to die hating you." Anna's voice broke as she said it.

"I don't want you to hate me!" Allie said.

"I don't," Anna said, shaking her head for emphasis even though she knew Allie couldn't see her.

"Well, good," Allie said. "I don't hate you either."

They laughed.

There was a pause, and then, at the same time, they both said, "I love you."

They cracked up again.

"Well, alright then," Anna said.

"Okay," Allie said. "You take care of you. And the kid. And the house."

"I will, sis," Anna said. "Don't worry. You worry too much."

And then she laughed again. Ever since they were kids, Allie had always been the one telling Anna to stop worrying so much.

Chapter 28

Sam had stopped treating Anna roughly in bed, and she missed it. One day, sitting at the computer in Allie's office, Anna turned to Sam as she walked by and pulled her over by the belt loop.

"Phoenix?" she asked Sam.

"Downstairs watching *Milo and Otis,*" Sam said. She walked over to the door and closed it. "It doesn't lock. But the movie just started, he'll be down there for a while."

"Let's go out to the hot tub," Anna said. It was the middle of the day, but no one could see them.

With a sultry nod from Sam, Anna pulled off her sundress, draped it around her lover's neck. Started outside, pulling her forward. Then making sure Sam was following, watching.

She climbed into the tub slowly, flexing her shoulders. Testing her wings. They were healed and now she could go in the water again.

She made sure Sam was still watching, admiring her handiwork. The salt-and-pepper wings that were Sam's first, second, only tattoos on her body.

Sam pulled off her clothes and climbed into the water behind Anna. She sat, pulling Anna into her lap, Anna's legs straddling her. Sam took one of her nipples in her mouth, then the other. Her thumb found Anna's clit and her hand found her opening. She reached inside.

"Harder," Anna said in her ear.

After they had both come, they stayed in the tub. It was the only place, other than bed, where Anna felt comfortable now. She stretched her happy, naked, high-on-Oxy body out in front of her, and Sam held her up, her hand in the small of Anna's back, and spun her gently in circles. Anna watched the trees above her turn like a kaleidoscope, light streaming through their branches. Her hair was dark with water and it spread out around her torso, through the water, like seaweed.

The chlorine smell was totally gone now, since they hadn't added any since they got there. Anna had seen some algae forming at the bottom, but it was better than chlorine. *Let it go wild,* she thought. She hoped Allie wouldn't be too upset that she hadn't taken care of it like Allie told her to.

Anna closed her eyes. She said, "Can we use these last weeks to do everything we want to do together? You, me, and Phoenix. Can we do that? Can we make a list?"

"Yes." Sam pulled Anna's head gently out of the water and over to hers, and kissed her. "I haven't made any tat appointments this month yet, I'll just tell Dustin I can't work. I want to be with you."

"You can work. You don't have to spend every day with me."

"Let's see. Let's write our list and go from there."

"Okay. Want to do it now?"

"Yeah," Sam said. She kissed Anna again and then got out and quickly dried off, wrapping her towel at the hips. She grabbed Anna's towel and Anna swam over to her.

The warm evening air blessed Anna's naked skin. Sam held her and dried each part of her, slowly and carefully. "My mermaid."

Once they were dressed, Sam went downstairs to get Phoenix. "Bring your sketchbook and markers," Anna called down.

He clomped up the stairs and into the kitchen, looking sleepy, and put his sketchbook and markers on the table.

"Come here, bud," Anna said. He walked over and climbed into her lap. *What if this is the last time I can hold him like this?* She was barely able to tolerate his weight, which was probably about equal to hers now. He was oblivious to her discomfort, though, and she was glad about that. "We want to write a to-do list. But not of boring work things—a list of fun things we want to do together. Will you be the official writer-downer?"

"Okay," he said, brightening a little.

"And we need your help thinking of things," Sam said. "I have one, can I go first?"

Anna and Phoenix nodded.

"I want to paint your portrait," Sam said to Anna, tears pooling into her eyes.

"Okay," Anna said, reaching out to take Sam's hand.

"Painting of Mama," Phoenix said and wrote it down.

"Wow, good job, Phoenix," Anna said, raising her eyebrows at Sam.

<u>To Do</u>

   1. Painting of Mama (S)
   2. Go zip-lining (A)
   3. Go on a roller coaster (P)
   4. Go to New York City (A)
   5. Volunteer at animal shelter (A, S, P)

6. Take Sam to the daisies (A, P)
7. Go to the opera (A)
8. Make a movie (A)
9. Have a big party (S)

It seemed like the list should have a nice round ten items, but they left space in case they thought of something else.

The thing that Anna wanted most, she didn't want to say out loud. It was too important, too vulnerable. And she wouldn't be the one who would make it happen. She just had to trust.

Chapter 29

*T*he party was Sam's idea. She wanted to share Anna with all the people they loved, to open their life up to the world for a night. With the support she was getting from the blog, things had started to feel more expansive, like they weren't alone in this. She wanted Anna to have that feeling too—that they would be okay, after she was gone.

Sam's mom would cook, and the person who'd been spinning the night they went dancing would DJ. They could invite the friends they'd made in the neighborhood; they could wait until the twins and Leo and Allie were back so they could be there too.

"We could invite Claire and Skyla to come up," Anna said. She had still not told Claire about her diagnosis; she had hedged after her appointment with the neurologist, and Claire hadn't pressed for details.

"Yes! Great. I want you to have fun, though, so will you let me take care of all the details?"

"Okay. No champagne for me, though, after what happened at Pix."

"No. Margaritas?"

"Mmm, that sounds good. We could have a fiesta. A fiesta pool party. Just trash Allie's house."

They laughed.

"In that case," Sam said, "can I invite some of my skater

friends? I've been wanting to introduce you to them. And the guys from the tattoo shop."

"Anyone you want. Just not my parents. I don't need that drama."

"Your parents are not invited."

"Allie offered to call them for me. But I don't know. I just can't imagine that would go well."

"I'll just say one thing: No regrets."

"I know. I'm thinking about it. But the thought of talking to her is upsetting. I don't need that right now."

"No, you don't. But if Allie told her for you…who knows, you might get an apology out of her. That could be good, right?"

"I guess. Okay, I'll tell Allie about the party. When should we have it? They're getting back the 29th."

"How about Saturday the 31st? Olivia will be here then, she can help. How's that sound?"

"Okay. Good talk." Anna moved in toward Sam on the couch, let herself be held. Her arms had lost most of their strength, and even hugging required more energy than she had most days.

"I'm proud of you," Sam said. She knew that if it were up to Anna, it would be just the three of them, until the end.

"Thanks," Anna said.

She was quiet then. *Is it time to talk about it? The end?*

She turned away so that her back was up against Sam's chest, Sam's arms still around her. Sam was nuzzling her nose in Anna's hair.

Anna said, "I don't want to say goodbye to you and Phoenix. I want you guys there with me when I go, but I don't want to say goodbye."

"Okay." Sam was quiet. "Do you know where you want to be?"

"No. No, I can't think about that yet."

"No worries. Take your time. I just want you to get everything you want."

They went back to the doctor for the second visit. When Anna described her symptoms—the worsening headaches, a bad fever a couple days before, drowsiness and nausea—he said it sounded like a turn for the worst.

"Of course I can't say how long it will be before things get really bad," he said. "No one can predict that."

She knew this, of course, because the neurologist had told her she had six months or less, and it had been much longer than that already.

"It's not an exact science, unfortunately," the doctor said. "Have you had trouble breathing?"

Anna nodded.

"I would say it's a matter of weeks then. Not months."

"Will you prescribe the Seconal today?"

"Yes."

"Good, then we'll have it."

"Yes. Do you think you'll want help administering it? There are volunteers from Compassionate Choices who can come and help."

"No," Sam said. "I can do it."

"Are you sure?" Anna asked.

Sam nodded. "Just tell me what to do."

"Well," the doctor said, "you'll break open the tablets, mix what's inside with water, and Anna, you'll need to drink it down quickly, so that you don't get too tired to take it all. You can have a chaser of whatever you want afterward, to get rid of the taste; it will be very bitter."

"Then what will happen?"

"Within a few minutes, you'll slip into a coma. At some point after that, usually a couple hours or less, you'll be gone."

Anna and Sam looked at each other, and then at the doctor. Anna grabbed Sam's hand. "Okay," she told the doctor. "That's what I want."

"Okay. I'll refill the other scrips too, the Oxy and the anticonvulsant. They seem to be working well for you. You haven't had any convulsions, have you?"

"Not since I started taking the anticonvulsant."

"If you want it, if you get to that point, morphine is also an option. You would need someone to come and administer it."

"No, I don't want that," Anna said. "No offense, but I don't want any medical people around. When the pain is more than I can handle with the Oxy, it will be time to go. That's how I'll know."

"That's helpful, to have a clear sign that it's time. That will make your decision easier. Do you have all your paper-work and things in order?"

"Yes," Anna said. "And we told my son. Our son." She fought back the tears that bristled against her eyes when she said this. Her throat ached. "Well, we told him I'm sick, anyway. Not about the pill. Not yet."

"Wonderful," the doctor said. "Good for you."

"We wrote a bucket list with him," Sam said. "Next is New York City. Anna's never been."

"Oh, wonderful," the doctor said again. "Will you be taking your son?"

"We should, right?" Anna said to Sam.

"Definitely."

"Can we stay at a fancy hotel?" Anna asked.

"Nothin' but the best for you, baby," Sam said.

Chapter 30

*S*o they stayed at the Plaza for four glorious nights. Mostly Anna was too weak to do much. In the airport they'd had to have one of the flight attendants call a little cart to take them down to baggage claim, which Phoenix had loved.

But Anna could see Central Park from the room—they were on the seventeenth floor and she felt like she could see all of New York. She loved to gaze out the window. In the mornings, she encouraged Sam and Phoenix to go for a walk in the park and she would watch them as they came out of the hotel and onto the street; they'd wave to her, and they couldn't see her, but she waved back anyway.

She fought her regret at not being able to see the city, now that she'd finally made it here. She saved her energy for when Phoenix was around, and for seeing *Mary Poppins* and *La bohème.*

It would be enough. It had to be.

Anna took lots of video in the room, while they were out, and Phoenix and Sam did too, and then they shared what they had seen and done when they were returned to each other.

Sam told Anna she had a surprise for her. They took a cab from the hotel, a short distance away. Pulling up to a modest brownstone, Anna looked at Sam with a comical confusion.

"Do *you* know what we're doing, bud?" she asked Phoenix, and he nodded. He looked like he was about to burst but kept his mouth closed, his big brown eyes bright with excitement.

"Is it something from the list?" Anna asked, totally clueless.

Sam and Phoenix just shook their heads. They got out and helped her onto the sidewalk, then into the lobby of the building and into an elevator. *Still no clue.*

When the elevator doors opened, a petite, effervescent woman greeted them. She looked familiar, but Anna couldn't place her.

She introduced herself. "Hi Anna, I'm Samuelle. I'm Sam's godmother."

As Sam and Samuelle hugged for what seemed like forever, Anna remembered where she recognized the woman from: the Samuelle Couture website. Those beautiful, angelic dresses. *That's right, she lives and works in Manhattan. But what are we doing here?*

Sam, reading her mind, said, "I wanted you to meet Auntie Sam. After my mom, she's my most important family."

Samuelle led them to a little sitting area, then sat down on a love seat next to Phoenix. "Hi there. Who are you?"

Phoenix looked over at Anna, a little hesitant. She smiled, encouraging him.

"I'm Phoenix," he said, raising one eyebrow. He had dressed up for the occasion, wearing long pants, which rode up to reveal the custom high-top Vans that he and Sam had picked up on arriving in the city, which they had designed together on the website back in Portland. They were especially made for skateboarding, extra durable, with super-sticky soles and enhanced stability and support in the heel. He had picked out a red checkerboard for the tongue, toe, and main part of the shoe. The laces and side stripe were yellow and the sole featured red, yellow, and orange flames.

He was so proud of them, the first time he had designed something himself, and Anna loved them too, though his feet looked enormous to her. He was developing his own style, growing up before her eyes. Even though she was with him every day, the growing gaps in her short-term memory meant that she experienced him like someone who saw him intermittently. She had to remind herself that he was six years old now. In her mind, he was still four. Where had her silly boy gone?

Samuelle showed them around the studio, and Anna delighted in all of the dresses—dozens of them, many more than they had seen on the website—plus all of the luxurious fabrics and notions, ribbons, jewelry, tiaras.

And then they arrived at the Cecile: the dress Anna had fallen in love with, at Sam's mom's kitchen table. It graced a dress form in front of her, far prettier than in the pictures on the website. The simple, lovely bodice was made of Chantilly lace with a hand-cut applique. The skirt was silk charmeuse and hung almost casually to the floor.

"Would you like to try it on?" Samuelle asked, and Anna found herself nodding, caught up in the fantasy. Sam and Phoenix moved away, to give them some space.

When Samuelle had helped her into the dress, pinning back the extra fabric so that it fit perfectly, she led Anna out to the viewing area, which featured a raised platform with mirrors that showed every angle. But Anna made a beeline for her loved ones.

Sam stood, nervously waiting, as Anna walked toward her.

Nearing Sam, Anna remembered their first date, how her platform sandals had made her Sam's height. Anna kissed Sam, now, and they didn't worry about the others. Sam held Anna's precious head in her hands and kissed her mouth, her eyes, her cheeks. Barefoot now, Anna was a little shorter than her, the dress trailing behind her, and Sam pulled away, with great effort, to inspect her.

One might have assumed that the dress would play up her paleness, her delicacy—that it would complement Anna's thin arms, her exquisite collarbone.

Instead, Anna had never looked more alive. Something had transformed in her. Maybe it was just the magic of the dress, but Anna seemed enlivened. Like the Cecile had given her energy.

She had color in her cheeks and an impish grin as she looked over at Phoenix. He walked up to them, stood at Sam's side, and watched her shyly, with a kind of reverence.

Of course he has changed. Everything has changed, she thought.

"There's something else, Anna," Sam said, distracting her from her musings.

Sam and Phoenix stood across from her, and they were holding hands now. She stood and watched them, and they watched her.

"What is it?" Anna asked quietly.

"Your fitting. That's what's next."

"For what?" Anna asked.

"For the dress, Mama," Phoenix said.

Samuelle walked over to them. "We already pretty much did the fitting, I can base it on the adjustments I made to this floor model. I have these fabrics in a lot of different colors, I'll help you choose one. And then I'll sew it for you. Quickly, so you'll have it for the opera, and can take it with you when you leave."

Anna was stunned and Sam and Phoenix smiled, pleased with themselves. Sam's namesake efficiently whisked Anna away.

They effortlessly avoided all things bridal, choosing together a sage-green satin and matching lace that were glorious against Anna's evanescent skin. Samuelle couldn't have gushed over Anna more if she had been a bride-to-be, circling her on the mirrored platform, pinning and making notes as Sam and Phoenix watched quietly. They decided to make the skirt much shorter, so it would skim the floor, rather than trailing along it. Anna had packed some high-heeled boots that she thought would work perfectly.

Auntie Sam would do a week's worth of work in a day, so that Anna could wear her lovely creation in the city that had inspired it.

PHOENIX

Guess what, we went to New York! We stayed in the Plaza Hotel, which is a famous place where a girl in a book lived. Her name is Eloise. When Mama was little she read the books, and it made her want to go to New York and stay in the Plaza Hotel, so that's what we did! We pretended we were rascals like Eloise.

Mama wasn't feeling very well because the lump in her head is getting bigger. So she couldn't go out much. Sam and I went to Central Park, to a pond with remote-control boats, to a playground and carousel. We played chase through the trees. Sam is good at being like a kid, luckily, since Saffron is not talking to me.

But after a while we would start to miss Mama and we would go back to the Plaza Hotel to eat. Usually we got room service, but a couple times we went out. Mama doesn't eat much anymore but Sam usually eats all of her food and whatever Mama doesn't eat AND whatever I don't eat!

We didn't bring our skateboards to New York but I know Sam wished we did. Everywhere we went she talked about what it would be like to skate there. But she said we'll go back another time and bring our boards.

I don't like talking about Mama not being here. I am trying to be brave but thinking about it makes it harder.

Oh, and the best part was we went to see *Mary Poppins* on Broadway, and at the end Mary flew over the crowd! She flew right over my head! I waved to her, and she waved back.

Also, I went on my first roller coaster! At Coney Island.

It was called the Cyclone. Sam said it is one of the most intense roller coasters in the world and she couldn't believe how brave I was. She went on it with me and took video of the whole thing to show Mama.

I closed my eyes for the whole time, so I was glad to see the video later. It looked even more scary than it felt. But Sam laughed through the whole thing and that made us laugh too.

Chapter 31

*I*t was good that they went to New York when they did, because after their return Anna started getting dizzy spells. A couple times she passed out. Another time, she missed the cue that she had to go to the bathroom and was unable to make it to the toilet in time. She now felt unsafe driving, or even walking on the street more than a block or two.

It was happening, and Anna started getting clinical about her death, as if she was the manager of it. They moved the party up to Friday the 23rd. Anna asked Allie to come back early, and they arranged to be back on the 20th, the same day Olivia was arriving. Allie's family would stay nearby so Olivia could stay at the house.

Anna and Sam and Phoenix had chosen a new school for him—a Waldorf school in San Francisco's Pacific Heights. They were saving a spot for Phoenix, but school started Monday, August 26. Anna wanted them to get back in time for Phoenix to make it to his first day of first grade.

Anna decided on Saturday, August 24, as her death day. The moon would be full and waning.

Sam and Phoenix would drive back on August 25, and the following day Phoenix would start at his new school. It would be a lot for Sam and Phoenix to deal with, but Anna and Sam agreed that it would be best for them to keep busy. Sam had accepted Joey's job offer to manage the new tattoo parlor, and they'd even found a furnished sublet in the Richmond district, near the beach, that Sam and Phoenix would move right into, until they could deal with their houses in the East Bay.

For the party, Sam coordinated a Mexican menu with her mom and rounded up blenders and tequila for margarita-making. She put Phoenix to work making *papel picado*—brightly colored tissue paper that he cut shapes out of, like snowflakes; they would string them together and hang them all over. Sam also found some multicolored Christmas lights in the garage, and with Phoenix's help hung them in the backyard trees, and in the living room and kitchen. They started using them instead of the regular lights, to help with Anna's headaches, which were pretty constant now. The lights gave the house an enchanted quality that suited the strange limbo they were all in.

Maybe it's just the Oxy, she told herself. But she saw that Sam and Phoenix too were looking at her differently, looking at everything differently. Every second was important. Everything they did had meaning.

Anna was listening to her favorite Russian novels on audio, and this too lent a strange fantasy to the house. Were they in 1800s Russia? Was she Anna Karenina, reincarnated? As she drifted between sleeping and waking, she wasn't sure who or what she was. Maybe that was good, though, since soon she would be something else.

Sam read to her from *Many Lives, Many Masters*—hoping that maybe the groundbreaking exploration of reincarnation would help Anna understand what was going to happen after she died, make it less scary. She skipped around, only reading the parts that seemed helpful.

"This is actually really helping me," Sam told Anna. "Maybe we'll get to know each other again, in another life."

"Maybe," Anna said quietly. Her breath was shortened, making it hard for her to speak loudly. "Hey…"

Sam leaned in close, and Anna continued. "I think I know where I want to…do it," she whispered. "I want to show you the field of daisies. I think that's where I want to be. When I die."

Anna swallowed, caught her breath, closed her eyes. "Lying in the daisies and looking up at the sky."

Anna was afraid but made herself open her eyes and look at Sam. Her expression was unreadable.

So Anna pushed on. "Can we do that? Will you go with me?"

"Of course. That's what you want? Are you sure?"

Anna nodded. "What I want. On a big, soft white blanket. You holding one hand, Phoenix the other."

"We can do that, love," Sam said quietly, her voice breaking. But her eyes stayed dry.

Chapter 32

Once her husband and kids were settled in at their Airbnb around the corner, Allie went home to see Anna and get them all some new clothes. Anna met her at her front door and welcomed her in with an ironic flourish. Sam had taken Phoenix with her to pick up her mom at the airport, so Anna and Allie could have some time together. Anna hadn't said why, just that it was important.

Her most important thing.

In the bedroom, Allie swapped out her dirty clothes for clean ones. Despite her clarity around wanting to make things right with her sister, Anna felt disoriented by Allie's presence. The strange spell of this weird new liminal reality was broken by her sister taking her rightful presence in the room that Anna had almost started to think of as her own.

Wait, what's happening now? Anna's head spun and she sat on the bed.

Guessing that Anna was about to insist that they stay here, at home with them, Allie shushed her. "This is good, Anna, I'm happy you're here. The house isn't big enough for all of us, and you're all settled in."

Anna looked around the room, at her clothes hanging from doorknobs. Quietly, she said, "This may be morbid but…if I wash them, can I leave my clothes here with you? You can do whatever you want with them, donate, or.…"

Allie nodded with a small smile. "Okay, but…do me a favor and don't wash them? I don't know, I just feel like… maybe it will be nice having you around a little longer." She shook her head, cheeks reddening.

Anna stood, feeling a little shaky, and walked to the closet, pulling out the garment bag. "I don't have much, so I'm afraid this will be your inheritance." She tossed it onto the bed, then sat down again. "Hope it fits."

Allie pulled the Cecile from its sheath and her jaw dropped. "What is this?"

"Sam's godmother, Samuelle, is a dressmaker in New York. She made it for me while we were there." After taking a sip from her bedside water glass, Anna said, "Try it on. I want to know if you'll be able to use it."

"Anna," Allie croaked, her voice rough with emotion. "No. Where would I even wear it?" Allie sat heavily down on the bed.

Anna moved to the carpet in front of her and pulled off Allie's shoes, then tugged down her skinny jeans. Allie allowed her sister to undress her, then slip the fine fabric over her head.

The dress fell right into place, settling onto Allie's hips snugly, suggestively.

Anna swallowed. *This is what the old me would have looked like in it.* She couldn't help thinking that Sam would have preferred this, her sexy sister, who looked sultry in the garment, where Anna looked see-through, half-gone. She was glad that Sam wasn't there to see.

She spun Allie around and slowly zipped her up. "It fits you better."

Allie smoothed out the silk, fluffed the tulle, and spun.

"Hey, I bet that means you have a bathing suit that would fit me," Anna said. "I've been going in the hot tub every day and I'm sick of mine. Don't be mad but I haven't been using *quite* as much chlorine as you suggested."

"Anna!" Allie looked like her sister again, hands on hips in irritation.

"Don't worry, it's fine. Anyway, can I borrow a swimsuit for the party?"

Allie went to her dresser and gathered them all up into two big handfuls, tossing them on the bed next to the garment bag.

Anna started to check them out. "That's what I'm talking about," she said. When they were in high school the girls had shared clothes, but her sister rarely had anything she liked, being younger and more conservative. Now, Anna happily sat back against the pillows, pulling the bikinis to one side and the one-pieces to another.

Allie was admiring herself in the closet mirror, twisting her hair up, trying on a pair of stilettos. "My goodness, Anna. This is way nicer than my wedding dress."

Anna smiled, eyeing the tops and bottoms. "Aloha," she said sarcastically as she held up a couple tropical bikinis.

"Shut up," Allie said. "But yes, I definitely did buy those in Oahu when they lost my luggage."

"Pretty cute actually."

They were in their own worlds, together, in the hush of the house. No kids, no partners, no parents. No one but each other. Probably that hadn't happened since they were little.

This.

Anna had gained the most extraordinary ability to notice things in the moment that they were happening. To be quiet, and notice. To not want more.

This, now, with my sis.

Their last time together in this lifetime was only going to add up to a few hours.

Burdened not just by the scarcity of their future but by the inadequacy of their past, Anna wanted to do all the things: show Allie Phoenix's artwork, make her a cocktail, go out to the hot tub and show her the moss growing there. Make her dinner. Make her laugh. Tell her a story. Ask to see pics of Violet and Dahlia. Take pictures of *her*, in the Cecile.

Instead, she stayed. Savored the bright patterns and colors, amused by the complex designs, impressed and pleased at Allie's surprisingly large collection.

And then, finally, at the bottom of the pile, Anna came upon a sage-green one-piece. It had a deep low V in the front and a delicate web of ties in the back. Elegant and simple, like the Cecile.

She slipped out of her shorts and top and investigated the complex holes, pulled it on. She walked over and stood in front of Allie at the mirror, let her sister tie up the strings in the back, tightening them a little until it fit Anna perfectly.

Anna turned to look at her butt. "Pretty good," they both said at the same time.

And it was. Anna's butt looked great in the bathing suit, as if it had been made for her.

Allie turned too, and they both looked over their shoulders, checking their asses out. Allie let out a loud wolf whistle and Anna doubled over, laughing.

"How did you do that?" she asked her younger sister. She had always wanted to learn how, thought it was so badass every time someone, especially a woman, let one loose.

"You just put your fingers to your lips and...blow," Allie said in her best Lauren Bacall.

Chapter 33

*A*nna spent most of her party holding court in the hot tub. The sunny day was beautiful, the warm evening divine.

Their new DJ friend stayed all day, serving up a dancey, trancey mix of hits and deep cuts. People danced, ate, soaked. They came and left and came back again. Sam had placed some big slabs of plywood she'd found against the fence, for Phoenix to practice on, and her friends joined him, gave him pointers.

Olivia kept the food table full of fresh tortillas, guacamole, and salsa. Phoenix helped her. The colorful paper flags he'd made created a friendly, celebratory vibe.

He's quite the host, Anna thought. Despite the fact that, she realized now, she and Phoenix had never had a party before—not once. *He needs people around him. Sam will make sure he has that.*

Anna kept visiting the website of Phoenix's new school. It seemed too good to be true, so Anna tried to imagine him in the pictures too, his body growing into the empty spaces. Happy, fulfilled, proud. It was painful to see him like that, without her, sitting under eucalyptus trees, in a place so different from the urban public-school chaos they were used to—but she knew it would be just the thing. He would be someone else's student, not hers, and with the school's low student-to-teacher ratios, he would receive so much more attention, would have access to so many more resources.

Anna had to admit that the only real reason she had taught at Peralta was to get Phoenix a spot at the school (a coup for a family outside the neighborhood, its arts and academics among the best Oakland had to offer), and to be with him there. But she didn't love teaching; she loved the kids but not the work. Phoenix deserved better, and now he would have it.

Claire and Skyla hadn't been able to make it to Portland. Anna had had an emotional, strained phone call with Claire instead. Now she was glad Claire wasn't there. The last thing she needed right now was awkwardness. She felt she could be herself around everyone who had come, even the people she didn't know.

She sipped her margarita, which was blessedly not causing any pain or nausea. Her hair was wet, curling into ringlets. Allie's sage-green suit was comfy and Anna had caught Sam looking at her with desire. They hadn't had sex since the time in the hot tub, which had to be weeks ago now.

Sam was wearing a dark blue sleeveless shirt and a new pair of black jeans. Catching Anna's eye, Sam excused herself from a chat and walked over, smiling. "How you doing, babe?"

"I'm great," Anna said drunkenly as she turned around slowly, sunk her shoulders against the jets.

Sam said, "Excellent. The margaritas are doing the trick."

"Yeah," Anna said into the bubbles. "But it's everything."

"When are you guys heading back to the Bay?" asked one of the skaters, who was sitting next to Anna in the tub.

"Oh, haven't you heard?" Anna asked smoothly. "I'm killing myself tomorrow."

All eyes in the tub turned to Anna. "Jungle Boogie" was playing over the jets.

"Yep. I want to go out on my own terms. It's why we came to Portland."

Across the tub, Allie put her finger to her mouth, shushing her, but it was too late. Anna heard her son's voice from behind her: "Why did we come to Portland?"

She closed her eyes. She was afraid she would pass out if she turned around to see him. Instead she put her arms up for him, like you would for a baby. *Give him to me.*

Phoenix pulled off his lime-green T-shirt, handed it to Sam, and climbed into the tub. Anna pulled him into her lap.

She looked into his eyes, which she had often wished looked like hers—or, better, that hers looked like his. But now, suddenly, she realized that Phoenix's bright brown eyes looked, very much, like Sam's. Perhaps Sam's soulful brown eyes had reminded Anna, in those early infatuated days, of her son's.

Looking into Phoenix's eyes, no matter the color, was like looking into her own soul. This part of her was going to live on.

Now she saw Sam in them too. They would be each other's now, with their beautiful eyes and their cool skateboards.

Sam leaned up against Anna's back, outside the tub, there if they needed.

Anna knew she needed to answer Phoenix's question. She didn't care who heard. There wasn't enough time to curate everything. He was surrounded in love and she was not ashamed of the way out that she had chosen, the empowered choice she was privileged to have.

She swallowed, found his hand under the water, and squeezed. He looked at her, eyebrows knitting, anger beginning. Another thing she'd be leaving Sam to deal with, and it wasn't fair.

Anna had to try and find a way to tell him the truth. "I'm gonna fly away from here, bud. You're the phoenix, but I'm—"

"What? How are you going to fly?" he asked.

Her voice scratching, her heart like a rock stuck in her throat, Anna said, "With a magic pill."

"Are we coming?" Phoenix asked, and now Anna's heart threatened to come up and out of her.

Or the tumor—trying to escape, blocking her words.

Phoenix was watching her. He was testing her. He was six years old. Not little anymore, no longer a toddler. He pushed himself off her lap. Standing in front of her, he was taller than she was, where she sat against the side of the tub.

The jets were making her back itch. She pressed the button to turn them off and the tub was suddenly silent. In addition to Sam's friend and Allie, who were in the tub with Anna and Phoenix, Olivia and Joey had walked over, and stood outside next to Sam.

Be calm. Be clear.

"No, you can't come with me." Anna cleared her throat. "The pill is only for people who are very sick."

She held her hand out in front of him and squeezed it together, making a little fountain.

Then, after a few minutes, she tried to wolf whistle, to no avail. Allie said quietly, "You just have to find the sweet spot, sis. You're almost there."

Phoenix tried, then Sam, but no one could do it like Allie, whose kids came running as if summoned and both climbed into the tub. Joey and Olivia got in too.

The sun started to go down and Sam turned on the

lights. The DJ announced "This one is for Anna, from Sam" and played the Yeah Yeah Yeahs' "Warrior." People flailed and shook their heads, and their shadows flung color all around the yard, up into the trees.

As Allie put one arm around Dahlia and the other around Violet, Anna felt a shock of love: for her two lovely nieces, for her sister. She had stayed away from them for too long.

Anna thought, *Please don't go, Allie. Please don't say it's time for you guys to go. Not yet.*

Then Sam came back, and kissed her on the cheek.

This lover. The love of my life. Most people don't ever get a love like this.

"I love you guys!" Anna yelled suddenly, and then she laughed, at how silly she had become. How glorious it was to let it all go.

Someone snapped a photo, and when Anna tugged Sam closer for a kiss, Joey reached out and pulled Sam into the tub with them. Sam came up laughing, dunking Joey, then floated to Anna and scooped her up.

"We love you too," Sam said, then, into her ear, "You're the prettiest girl here."

Then they kissed, a deep, heavy kiss. Anna pulled her sunglasses off and threw them into the yard, and some- one picked them up and carefully placed them on the food table. Allie pulled Phoenix over to play patty-cake with the girls, and Joey and Olivia averted their eyes, started a conversation with the skater, so Anna and Sam could kiss.

They kissed, and kissed, and kissed some more. Anna wanted to plunge her hand into Sam, under the water.

"Later," Sam said in her ear. "You just wait."

Chapter 34

*A*nna, Phoenix, Sam, Allie, and Olivia left early the next morning for the coast. Sam drove the Prius. There were things on their to-do list that hadn't gotten done, but Anna felt okay about it. In the passenger seat, an old white cotton sundress soft against her skin, Anna found that all she wanted to do was look out the window, holding Sam's hand.

No music. Music hurt too much now, added to everything else she was losing.

La bohème was stuck in her head, from the movie they'd made of their trip to New York, which they'd shared at the party the night before. Sam had surreptitiously recorded audio of the opera, and the arias played behind images of Central Park, all the places Phoenix and Sam brought back to Anna when she couldn't join them. The sculpture park overlooking the East River. Phoenix running to catch a subway train, squeezing in just before the door closed with a victorious fist pump.

Their room at the Plaza. Jumping on the bed.

Anna in her special dress—modeling it for Samuelle post-delivery, at the window looking out at the city lights. Sam in the background, sketching her.

The Cyclone, Phoenix's first roller coaster. Phoenix with his eyes shut and Sam's laughter mixing with the crash of the Atlantic behind them.

In front of the ornate opera house, with its arched doorways, decorative masks of comedy and tragedy. Anna's first opera, and Phoenix's too, *La bohème* was love at first sight, for them as for the protagonists.

Rodolfo and Mimi meet. Rodolfo sings to her about his poems.

Then she gets sick, and Mimi tries to leave him. They agree to stay together until spring, when the world will bloom again.

When Mimi succumbs to illness, and then death, apparently Puccini himself was moved to tears.

On the way to the freeway, Sam took them by the skate park, where a new mural had been painted under the bridge: WE LOVE YOU, ANNA, in charming cursive. A few of the skaters had headed down together after leaving the party, to paint it under cover of night, in pink and orange, blue and green. *The same colors Phoenix cut his papel picado from*, Anna realized, touched.

Olivia, Phoenix, and Allie were squished in the back of the Prius, with Phoenix in the middle, which normally Anna would have deemed unsafe. But Phoenix knew that this was the day his Mama would die, and she wanted him surrounded by people who loved him.

He wasn't asking questions, but she knew it was because he didn't want to know any more, and she was glad, because she didn't want to tell him.

Two hours later, at the coast, Anna allowed Sam to come around and open her door, pulling her into a hug.

Her hair whipping in the wind, Anna smiled at her passengers from Sam's arms as they piled out.

This, she reminded herself.

They let go and walked over, holding hands, to where Olivia had found a big rock from which to look out at the sea. Anna wasn't going to be able to make it down to the water. She had almost no energy left and she needed to save it for the daisies.

The cliff where they sat felt so familiar to her; she seemed to remember looking up at it. When had that been—that time last summer? Were the dunes just right down there?

Had there been some kind of bird…?

But she couldn't hold the thought. The Oxy tugged it away.

Olivia took Anna's hand and petted it, gently, lovingly. Allie wrapped her arms around Phoenix, who sat in front of her.

After a couple minutes, Phoenix pointed out at the water. "Whale!"

No one else saw it at first, but then suddenly Anna saw a massive body crest.

"Oh, my god!" she said. "Phoenix, good eye! That's the first whale I've ever seen!"

First and only, babes. But I guess that's better than no whale.

"Promise me you guys will go to the ocean a lot," Anna said to Sam and Phoenix.

"We promise," Sam said. "Ocean Beach, a few times a week at least. It's only a five-minute skate from the new place."

Anna nodded. They would have San Francisco to explore, more whales to sight. Anna could easily imagine them at Ocean Beach together, where she and Sam had parked after their date at the hot tubs.

Something had happened there—was it their first kiss? No, that was at Sam's, after Anna fell in the grass.

It came to her like a gift that her brain had stored for this moment: Sam saying, "I have to tell you, I really like you." Sitting just like this, on Anna's left, eyes on the sea.

"I like you too," Anna had said.

She liked Sam still, so much—liked and loved and everything in between. Their love had been a honeymoon they had never had to leave.

They still lived in that bubble, and something about this made Anna feel like she wasn't going alone. This being was so close to her, they had never once turned away from each other in anger—not even she and Phoenix could say that. This being was so generous that she—they—wanted to give Anna exactly what she wanted, despite the heavy lifting (literally!) afterward.

Even the implications of moving her dead body was something they had been able to joke about. In Anna's memory, the field of daisies was in the middle of nowhere, but what if there were farmers with guns? They couldn't exactly just tromp through what could be someone's land with Anna's body rolled up in a blanket.

Anna was pretty sure that, as honeymoons went, theirs was both the weirdest and the best. The longest and the most fun, yes. The most depressing and the most ridiculous, definitely.

Pretty great sex too. It hadn't had time to get old, but Anna guessed it never would have. She thought Sam was just the hottest. She felt guilty about not understanding Sam as "they" until now; but then she reminded herself that Sam had only just figured it out. In fact, Sam had told her that she, Anna, had inspired Sam in claiming it, by clearly claiming her own right to a peaceful death. Hard to believe, but Anna would take it.

Their honeymoon had been packed full of growth, and undeniably cinematic. It had been drenched in richness and glory, going fast and getting strong, being brave and loving big.

The boy. Getting to be a family. *We will always have that. They will always have me. I'll be present, for a while at least. That will be honeymoon too.*

The honeyed moon, which she'd tracked from the stoop on Ruby Street after her diagnosis, the weed turning her eyes blurry, the moon's outline even seeming to quiver sometimes, to drip. She had watched it religiously—and, she realized now, that was something she had never told Sam. Not yet.

That was how they had kept the magic alive. There were so many stories still.

Her mind was busy, when they got back in the car, with remembering, trying to, the trip that she and Phoenix had taken the summer before. Where she had surprised him with the sea, after the dunes, and they had run down into it together. It was impossible how much had changed in one year. She longed suddenly for the simple days when it was just the two of them.

She looked at him in her visor mirror, in the back with his aunt and grandma, holding both of their hands, and her chest felt like it would explode. Death by love.

Love for Allie, a love that was unconditional, finally free of resentment. The knowledge that her sister loved her, and loved Phoenix, and would take amazing care of him if Sam ever couldn't. Love and admiration for Olivia, who would take great care of Sam.

Phoenix's family had more than doubled, in one year, even with losing Anna. If she'd gotten the diagnosis back when it was just them, what would she have done? She could almost understand those parents who kill themselves and their kids—the deep, dark overwhelm of no good options.

Having people in your life gives you options, she thought. *How did I not know this?*

She turned her mind to trying to remember. It had become a kind of meditation, a bedtime ritual where she let her mind rest in a field of white, home away from home. How she and Phoenix had gotten lost, how they'd found the daisies. She needed, now, to let them draw her in.

They left the GPS off, like it had been then. Anna had wanted to find her way without Sheila telling them what to do, and they would have to do the same this time. She just had to hope either she or Phoenix would recognize the turn. With her brain working the way it was, she couldn't be certain. Being unable to rely on her intuition was terrifying.

"Phoenix, tell me if you see where we turned when we found the daisies," she reminded him.

"The map, Mama!" Phoenix said suddenly. She loved that he called her Mama still, his attempt to rename her Mom having not stuck for more than a week or two. "You bought a map when we got lost."

"Oh, that's right!" she said, leaning forward carefully to open the glove box. "Good job remembering. Though we weren't lost."

Anna spread the map out on her lap and tried to find a landmark. All the lines converged and diverged, like swords piercing her temples.

She closed her eyes then, leaned back against the

headrest, clenched her fists against the pain. *My head is breaking. I'm breaking. Please make it stop.*

Allie said from the back seat, "Let me see that, sis."

Rolling her eyes, Anna shoved it back, unable to turn around.

Sam reached over, took Anna's hand and opened it, then closed it again. When Anna looked down she saw the familiar white pill in her palm.

She hadn't wanted to take any pain medication on her last day, to be clear-headed, but this wasn't clear. Sam was right. Sam handed her some water and Anna swallowed the pill. She turned back to the window and rested her head, holding Sam's hand.

A peaceful quiet came over the car on the bucolic, hilly drive. As her headache evaporated, Anna rolled her window all the way down and turned her face into the wind. All she wanted was to lie down in the daisies and feel the sun on her skin.

"There it is!" Phoenix shouted loudly, pointing to the right. "That's where we turned."

Sam, with super-speed reflexes, turned—though without slowing down, the Prius skidded a little. It felt to Anna like they went up onto two wheels and she widened her eyes at Sam. They were adding an action sequence onto the end of their honeymoon, and she loved it, but played it cool for the back seat.

"I remember the turtle at that park," Phoenix said excitedly, reminding Anna of his year-ago self. "I wanted to go but then we went away from it."

"We can go now," Anna said. "Let's go now."

"You sure?" Sam asked.

Sometimes the pills made her nauseous. Sam knew this. Were they pushing their luck to stop again?

Anna nodded. Sam pulled in and parked, and they all got out, the Prius having never before seen so much action. Luckily Olivia was small but Allie wasn't—they were all being gracious. She tried not to think of the drive home, what that was going to look like. Phoenix in the front (talk about unsafe) and her sister and Olivia in the back with her body. They had measured, Anna climbing in the back; she just fit, width-wise. It was going to be extremely awkward, but she had to trust it would be okay.

Anna pulled out the snacks she'd packed, including a lemon zucchini bread she'd baked, and set things out on a picnic table. She took Phoenix's hand, and walked slowly to the turtle.

It was a giant sea turtle, with a mosaic shell made of ceramic pieces. Its eyes appeared to Anna to be large globes, shining as if lit from within.

"You wanna swing, Mama?" Phoenix asked, and Anna nodded.

She let him take her arm, lead her to the swings. A few days earlier she had passed out and fallen, trying to walk too fast.

But they made it. She sat on a swing, and Phoenix sat on the one next to her.

He called out, "Sam! Will you push us?"

She was too weak to pump. Phoenix had known.

Sam ran over and gave them both a push, tickling Phoenix as he swung back to her, kissing Anna's neck dangerously, causing the swings to collide and go haywire, laughing that big, wonderful laugh.

Even holding on to the swing's chains took more energy than Anna had. *But I don't have to worry about falling and hurting myself. Not anymore.*

This was her last chance at one of her favorite pastimes.

She hooked her elbows around the chain and locked her hands at her chest.

"Higher!" Phoenix said, and Sam gave him a huge push.

"Higher!" Anna said, feet pointing back in their Converse, ruffled skirt flying up around her. She tucked it under her legs, as Sam pushed her higher.

"Higher?" Sam asked, and they both agreed. "Ma!" Sam called to Olivia, who was sitting snacking with Allie at the picnic table. "I need a hand!"

Sam focused just on pushing Anna, gently but firmly, checking in, until finally Anna could go no higher. She started to giggle at the thrilling drop that happened just before descent, and she looked over at Phoenix, who was laughing too.

His smile stretched across his face. She smiled big too as she blew past him, a rush of wind in between them, their hair blowing all around. It was exhilarating, going this fast, it felt wild and unsafe and she loved it. For once she wasn't worried about him; she knew he was safe.

Allie came over and got on the swing to Phoenix's left, and he tried to take her hand, but soon outpaced her and had to let go.

Olivia got on the swing to Anna's right. She didn't want to go too high, but Sam delighted in pushing her just slightly out of her comfort zone.

Allie let loose a wolf whistle into the wind, then Anna tried one too. Determined.

She was going to keep trying until she got this.

After, they took a picture of all of them sitting on top of the turtle, then piled back into the clown car. The wrong way was straight ahead.

Sam drove slowly, with Anna and Phoenix on high alert, watching for clues.

"We drove straight for a while, right, Phee?"

"Yeah," he said. "Probably about ten miles," he said to Sam. "Then I think we made a right."

Anna smiled. She had been over and over it in her head, and he'd known the way all along.

Eleven miles later, Anna saw a farm that she remembered, and next to it a crossroads, a street that only turned right. "Here," Anna said quietly, and Sam turned.

They drove for another mile, and then rounded a corner, and then there they were.

Daisies. A huge field full of them.

"We found them!" Anna said to whoops and applause from the back seat.

Sam parked at the side of the road. Anna pushed her door open and with great effort pushed herself out of the car, staring out at the sea of daisies, overcome with relief and gratitude. She had been afraid they wouldn't be able to find them, that she'd have to die in a sad hotel room somewhere. Now that they were here she could finally let go.

Her entire body awoke, every pore tingling. Fully alive again, like she hadn't felt in months.

"I love you guys," she said to Olivia and Allie, wanting now to be out in the daisies, alone with Sam and Phoenix. They had discussed how it would go: Allie and Olivia would stay with the car and make sure no one bothered them, and would help with Anna's body when it was over. Sam had done a quick assessment of the perimeter: no farmers, no guns.

They hugged her, together the three of them, then separately.

Anna said to Allie, gently, as she held her: "I don't blame you. For what happened with Mom." Allie's body shook with one giant sob, a great exhale, and Anna squeezed her. "It was what I wanted most, you know," she said to her sister. "To love you like this."

She pulled back and pushed her sunglasses up on her head, squinted at the sun. She looked into her sister's eyes, which were wet and red. "I love you so much."

Anna hugged Olivia next. "Thank you," she said into her shoulder. She pulled back, wanting to be sure Olivia could understand her. "Thank you for having Sam, and for raising her, them, to be such a good person, so that they can raise Phoenix to be a good person. That's all because of you."

"You're welcome," Olivia said, taking Anna's face in her hands. "I love you, you know." It was the first time she'd said it.

"I love you too," Anna said, nodding. She grabbed Olivia's hand, and her sister's hand, and held them for a moment, smiling at them. Then she squeezed them both and let go.

Sam had the backpack on and was staring out at the daisies blowing in the wind, holding Phoenix's hand. "Pretty sweet spot," Sam said as Anna walked over and took Phoenix's other hand.

She loved how this felt. A real family.

"Ready?" Sam asked.

"I am," Anna said, and Sam lifted the fence for her.

Chapter 35

Sam and Anna spread out the big white fluffy blanket as Phoenix ran through the daisies, which were mostly knee-height to him, some taller.

Once Anna was comfortable, Sam said, "I'm going to get this ready. So we have it when you want it."

Anna nodded, and closed her eyes. The sun was bright, just like she'd imagined, even with her big black sunglasses on.

"You're such a star," Sam said. "You're the star of my movie."

Anna smiled, and when Phoenix ran up to them, Sam quickly distracted him, handing him her phone. "Take a picture of your mama, will you? She looks so pretty."

Anna with her red lips, her silvery hair. White ruffles graced her shoulders and legs, their eyelet eyes like those of the daisies, a hundred tiny black holes. She slipped off her black Converse and her bare feet sought the side of the blanket, pressed down into grass and dirt.

Phoenix clicked several photos, then he and Anna lay down and took some selfies of themselves, from above. She hugged him to her and they lay there like that for a while, watching the clouds move above them, feeling the soft blanket beneath them.

From behind her, she heard a Mason jar lid being

twisted on. Her death dose was ready to go. It was up to her now. When, and how.

His body brought back, into her own, all the times she had held him close. Now he was holding her, and behind her she felt Sam do the same. She had thought that she would know when it was time, but now Anna didn't know how she would ever be ready to leave them.

Soon she wouldn't be able to walk anymore, though. She wouldn't be able to leave the house, and the pain would be unbearable. Better to go now, while things were still pretty good. Right?

She knew that was right. She wanted Phoenix to remember her like this, while she was fully present, even joyous. Her light had not dimmed—it would not have to.

Wanting it, and not wanting it. Wanting release, needing them more.

Anna turned onto her back, so that Sam's head on Anna's chest was less than an inch from Phoenix's face. They laughed to see each other at such close range.

All three lay back on the blanket then, and watched the clouds. *The clouds will tell me it's time,* Anna thought.

After a few minutes, she saw a shape in the clouds. "A whale!" she said to them. "Another one!"

The first hadn't been her last after all. She imagined herself up in the sky, swimming at its side.

La bohème was seeping out of Sam's phone, the illegal recording. Sam translated, "When the flowers bloom in spring, we'll have the sun as our companion."

The daisies seemed to nod in agreement, their bodies dancing. The daisies were all they could see. Daisies for days.

Days of daisies.

Anna squeezed Sam's and Phoenix's hands, three times each. *I. Love. You.*

Then she pushed herself up. She nodded at Sam.

Sam got the Mason jar and shook it. "It's going to taste bad, remember. We've got strawberry milk and chocolate milk as chasers."

"I'll take the strawberry," Anna said, opening the box of strawberry milk and setting it on the blanket in front of her, then opening the chocolate milk and handing it to Phoenix, where he sat. They made a little circle on the blanket.

She pointed to the Mason jar and said to Phoenix, "This stuff is going to fly me away, and it won't hurt a bit. Well, it will hurt my heart to leave you, but physically it will just be like I'm up there, swimming through the clouds."

Her voice broke, and she stopped. The pressure in her throat was unbearable, from holding back emotion.

"It's not going to hurt Mama, okay?" Sam tried. "It's just going to let her rest. We don't want her hurting anymore."

Anna said to him, "I'll be dreaming of you both as I go. So I'll be with you, still."

She turned to Sam, who was sitting cross-legged in front of her. She pulled her sunglasses off and tossed them away, into the daisies. This time there was no one to retrieve them, and they laughed.

Sam and Anna leaned in to each other and rested their heads together; Sam's forehead was cool against Anna's. "I'm so glad we got to show you the daisies," Anna said, taking Phoenix's hand.

"I am too," Sam said. "They are beautiful. Almost as beautiful as you."

"I'm so glad I got to know you," Anna whispered, looking into Sam's eyes. She had still never reached their end.

Honey sun, she thought. *Our honeymoon was a honey sun.*

"We were lucky," Sam said. "But now...we don't want you to suffer anymore."

Phoenix stood up, putting one arm around Anna and one around Sam, so that they were in a huddle. He said "Right," and it sounded to Anna like he believed it.

"Okay," Anna said, taking the jar from Sam.

Steady, but quickly, she reminded herself. The sedatives had to be drunk in under 60 seconds, so that she didn't pass out in the middle of drinking it and not take a lethal dose—but worse would be if she vomited it up.

She held the jar in her lap, moistened her lips, positioned her fingers against her mouth one last time. And blew.

A whistle rang out—not loud like Allie's, but louder than any sound she'd ever made before. Anna grinned proudly.

They waited.

A few seconds later, Allie's response returned: a loud, sharp whistle back.

She drank it all down then, and after the terrible aspirin taste she was grateful for the sweet, thick strawberry chaser.

She lay back down and held their hands again. Sam on her right and Phoenix on her left.

There was no time to be afraid. She said, "I left you guys something. It's on my computer desktop. I wrote it for you both. I hope you like it. Maybe you can illustrate it together, or sing it, or make it longer…it's not as long as I wanted it to be."

Anna's eyes were falling closed.

"Let's look at the sky for a while. Remember the whale? That's gonna be me…."

An "eee" from Mimi's farewell aria blended with Anna's last "me" and the tone entered her ears and spread deeper within, past and present and future all sustained in its bright pitch, carrying her.

Like whale song. Light faded and they called her in.

And then she *was* flying with them, swimming through

the ocean of her mind, past membranes, the tumor, water and brain and everything pulsing, pulsing, pulsing…and then slowing.

All of it coming to a stop, like a boat gliding into a dock.

Part 4:
The Sun

The Sun: A Fairy Tale

by Anna, for Phoenix and Sam

Once upon a time, there was a mermaid without a mother. For as long as she knew, she had been surrounded by her friends in the sea. It was her life, and she loved it. She never questioned it.

But as she grew, she began to wonder where she had come from. All the creatures she knew either had hatched from eggs, like her friend Elmer the sea dragon, or were birthed by their mamas, like her friend Sadie the whale shark.

Sadie's mother—who actually first had nourished Sadie in an egg within her body—fielded many questions from the mermaid on these topics. But most of the time she did not have the answers. She had never known another mermaid, and had no idea where the mermaid's parents had come from, or where she had come from. The mermaid was something of an anomaly, and while she felt protective of her, she couldn't give her what she was looking for.

The mermaid wondered what kind of mother she would like. Would she be large, or small? Would she have scales, or fur? She really didn't know what good qualities to have in a mother were, since she'd never had one.

Elmer didn't have a mother either. Once his mother had deposited him and 250 other eggs into his dad's tail, Elmer's dad had been their primary caregiver. Though that consisted only of carrying the eggs—since from the moment they hatched, the babies were completely independent—there was still quite a lot involved. His tail supplied the eggs with oxygen. They turned a bright purple or orange during this period (Elmer was orange), and after about nine weeks, Elmer's dad pumped his tail until the young emerged, slowly, over the next couple days. Elmer was one of the lucky 12 who had survived.

But his mother was nowhere to be found.

So Elmer joined the mermaid on her search for a mother. What will make a good mother? they asked each other. What are we looking for?

The traveled the sea in search of answers to these questions, having many adventures and growing quite close. Elmer was quite a bit younger than the mermaid, and she was able to teach him much of what he hadn't learned from his mother. She would tuck him into her tail and they would head off on their next quest.

Soon they forgot that they were looking. They were happy with what they had. It was then, when she stopped looking, that the mermaid realized: she didn't need a mother, she needed to *be* a mother. Being able to care for and teach Elmer had fulfilled her yearnings—this, she knew now, was the thing she had so deeply wanted and sought.

She realized that not having a mother had made her the strong, resourceful, silly, wild creature she now was, and it had also taught her generosity of spirit. She was able to give to Elmer without expecting anything in return. She grew to understand him better than she understood herself.

They developed a connection, a love, that was deeper than any the mermaid had ever known: a bond stronger than any kelp in the sea.

He named her Merrygold. They built their very own cave under the sea, decorated every nook and crook of the cave with things they found, then brought back home.

Sometimes she made her treasures into something else, like the seahorse skeleton she'd studded with sea glass, or the tiny houses she built out of fish bones. She slept in a kelp bed, in a corner of the cave.

Elmer just slept wherever; he would get tired and just go still, sometimes even for days at a time. Merrygold was used to her companion's quirks by now. Really, even though he had given her her name, he was more like her brother, or her son.

They may not have had mothers, but Merrygold and Elmer had many friends. During the day they roamed the sea on their own, doing their work, but at night they all came over, and many of them slept in the cave too. The sea stars, Stan and Sirius. The nudibranch, Brianna. The kelp snail, Norris, and the sea hare, Bunny.

Sea dragons, unlike their relative the seahorse, cannot curl their tails and hold onto seaweed to stay safe—and once, during a terrible storm, Elmer was washed ashore. After it had passed, Merrygold had searched everywhere for him, patrolling the waters and beaches until she found and saved her delicate friend, and brought him back to the cave to care for him, as he was very weak.

Leafy sea dragons usually live a solitary, sedentary lifestyle, but Elmer, once healed, probably traveled more than all the other leafies in the sea combined. It was like coming that close to death had made him invincible, insatiable. And though he was pretty slow—he used the tiny fins along the side of his head to steer and turn—she provided a wonderfully convenient, and fun, water taxi. If they caught the right current Merrygold didn't even have to really swim; the current would carry them. Or, if they wanted to go exploring in another neighborhood, they would ask a dolphin for a ride—they could swim much faster than she could.

Outside their cave, Merrygold had curated a coral garden. The seaweeds curved up and over its entrance, lending safety and privacy. The grasses also served to feed her friends: Norris especially loved the feather boa kelp. The beautiful sea plants bloomed the same blues and greens as Merrygold's tail, and more than once she had slipped into the garden to hide from a predator, or from someone she didn't feel like talking to, like the snapping shrimp—so loud!

Elmer was even better than Merrygold at camouflaging himself—he looked like seaweed to begin with, but also could change his color to blend in (as long as he had been eating well and wasn't too stressed out). This had come in handy many times, Elmer spying on one creature or another for Merrygold, acting as her lookout; he was so small and unobtrusive, often mistaken for seaweed even by creatures who should have known better.

Merrygold envied him. She had never had any privacy or obscurity; she could never in her life slip by unnoticed. She had never seen another like her in all her days, in all her travels.

She also made a swing, in the garden, out of the thallus of the Laminaria algae. In a ray of sun that beamed down in the afternoons, she spent hours swinging, watching the currents change and the animals cruise by.

When the light dimmed, she swam to the surface and watched the sun settle its shimmer across the sea as it left for the other side. She scavenged books from sunken ships and read them at night by the light of the bioluminescent fungi, phytoplankton, and glowworms in the cave.

It never occurred to her to leave the ocean. It was the only place she'd ever known, and its riches were far greater than she would be able to explore in her lifetime. She was not lonely, because she had Elmer, and the others. Though he was much smaller than she was.

Merrygold and Elmer both dreamed of flying. Merrygold studied the pelicans as they dove into and then out of the water, their mouths full of fish. Except for the part about eating fish (fish were her friends!), she wished it could be her. Sometimes when she was a little rascal she would grab on to the pelican's feet as they flew past and fly with them for a while before they shook her off. Eventually they started avoiding her when they saw her beneath the water.

She also loved to surf with the seals, and was close with some dolphins as well. When Merrygold was a merbaby, a dolphin named Linelle had looked after her, and for a time Merrygold had wondered if Linelle was her mother. Linelle even taught her how to whistle. There was a definite resemblance between them, with their similar coloring, and powerful tails; but as Merrygold grew she realized that they were more different than they were alike.

Speed, for one thing. Merrygold's body was built for leisurely exploring, but Linelle was built for efficiency. Elmer would hold tight to Merrygold and Merrygold would hold tight to Linelle and they would go fast, fast, fast. Linelle could jump out of the water, which both Merrygold and Elmer loved, so she did it now and then, to give them a thrill.

It was as close to flying as Merrygold and Elmer had ever gotten.

In Merrygold, eventually, a melancholy developed that

followed in her wake, a ghost that followed her like an invisible twin. Some days she sulked, wanting to be alone. Other days, when she was over being sad, she kicked at the melancholy with her powerful tail and tried to outrun the sadness.

But when she stopped moving, when she rested for the night, it always returned.

She ventured with Elmer further and further, until some nights they had gone too far to return to the cave to sleep. A couple times they slept in a sunken ship; another few times in a coral reef. It was no big deal for Elmer, and Merrygold learned not to need much by way of comfort.

One night they slept in a tidepool, surrounded by lava rocks. In the morning, Merrygold woke to a loud sound, one she had never heard before. It reminded her a little of the bellow of a whale, in its intensity; but it was higher-pitched and not muffled by the sound of the water, she realized. It was coming from land—from above her. From the sky?

Merrygold looked up. Above the beach where they had slept, at the top of a cliff, she could see a creature. It was hard to make out what it was; it was shadowed by the sun. But it looked to be about the same size as her.

Just as she went to wake up Elmer, to ask him if he knew what it was, the creature lifted off the ground and flew away in a great rush of beating wings. Merrygold moved closer, squinted to try and see, but it was soon gone, leaving her wondering, as she tried to explain to Elmer, whether her intense longing had manifested the mystery beast. It seemed far too big to fly.

That day, Elmer and Merrygold explored the tidepools.

In the afternoon, she got out of the water and rested on some rocks. Elmer was nervous that a human would see her. Humans were the sea animals' most-feared predator. Out of the water, Elmer couldn't protect Merrygold, and she couldn't protect him. She was able to be out of the water for hours at a time—maybe even days, though she'd never tried—but he couldn't survive on land for more than thirty minutes.

Merrygold and Elmer slept in the same tidepool as the night before, and Merrygold felt some nervous excitement as she drifted off. Would she dream of the great winged beast? Or would she wake in the morning to see it in the flesh?

Night came and the animals of the sea rested. When the sky started to lighten, Merrygold woke to the same cawing sound from the day before. It was definitely real, and it was definitely coming from a bird at the top of the cliff.

She could see it better this morning, as it was earlier in the morning and the sky was a soft pink. It looked to Merrygold—but how could that be? It looked like the bird had a brown body and a giant shimmering plume—feathers of the same iridescent blues and greens that Merrygold's tail was made of.

She climbed out of the water and sat on a rock, staring up at the creature in awe. With her toe she tried to wake Elmer, so he could see what she saw, but again, just as Elmer started to stir, the big bird seemed to leap up into the sky and took off with a great flurry of its magnificent feathers.

She described the creature to Elmer, and he, being very learned about land creatures, pronounced that the strange creature must have been a peacock. That was the only bird he knew of with such a fabulous plume. But it was curious, he said, because peacocks rarely flew even short distances.

The next morning, both mermaid and sea dragon were awake at dawn, and this time they stealthily crept along the beach and climbed the cliff. It was hard for Merrygold to climb with her unwieldy legs, which she rarely used, but with her strong upper body she was able to make it up the steep rocks, Elmer tucked gently under her arm. They had only a short window of time before Elmer would need to be back in the water, and they nervously awaited Peacock's return, hoping he would come soon.

Merrygold heard a rustling. She looked up at a giant oak tree, a ways back from the cliff, and it seemed to shiver. And then, from out of its branches, she saw the giant bird emerge. It didn't fly as much as glide down to the ground from the tree. Once on land, it preened a bit, seemingly performing some sort of morning ritual, its tail feathers pressed discreetly down.

Then it saw her. And froze.

Next thing she knew, its feathers were up and the cawing had started. She couldn't tell whether the grand bird was trying to impress her, or was scared of her. Maybe both? Merrygold thought it sounded like it was saying *Pea-cock! Pea-cock!*

It walked closer, but Merrygold and Elmer stood their ground. She felt self-conscious suddenly, her legs so inelegant, contrasted with the bird's brilliant beauty.

After watching it from afar, though, she felt an affinity forming, even though they had not yet met.

The following morning, Merrygold planted herself in the spot the peacock descended to each morning. When it arrived next to her, it landed heavily and then immediately pushed up its tail feathers, which fanned out, each one an intricate work of art. Merrygold stared, and the peacock stared back at her. How could they be so different from each other, and feel so much the same?

Back at the tidepool, she asked Elmer if he would want to leave the water for some time, if he could. She had heard stories of sea dragons who left the sea, to turn into land dragons.

Neither of them knew how it worked, but Elmer wanted to try. He wanted to stay with Merrygold, and he knew this was the only way.

So once again, in the morning, they scaled the cliff. They didn't really have a plan, but both felt maybe some kind of magic would occur up there, under the gaze of the mystical bird.

They waited for Peacock, and as they did Merrygold counted in her head the minutes Elmer had been out of the water.

15...16...

When she reached 25 they would be cutting it close. If Peacock hadn't arrived by then, if they were no closer to a transformation for Elmer, Merrygold would take him back to the water.

19...20...

The sun came up over the hill behind the oak tree. Merrygold heard a rustling in the tree that she knew by now was Peacock.

Hurry, she called to him in her mind.

22...23...

Elmer was not looking so good. Should she run

him down to the water now? They had never pushed his 30-minute limit on land. What if the limit was less than 30 minutes?

His body was dehydrating, like seaweed that had dried on a beach. His pretty yellow eyes looked glassy.

But Elmer wanted to wait.

Merrygold's heart was racing. She looked from Elmer, to the tree, waiting for Peacock. Surely they had passed 30 minutes on land now. She was afraid Elmer would die. But he wanted to stay.

And then, his eyes slid closed. His body dried up and withered into the dry grass beneath him.

"No!!" Merrygold screamed.

The peacock returned her call with one of his own and finally flew down to the ground, where she knelt.

Just as he landed, there was a tiny spark where Elmer's body had been. And then, before her eyes, emerged a tiny yellow dragon. He grew, and grew, his body expanding and his wings lengthening, until he was larger than Peacock.

He lowered his head to Merrygold, and she climbed on his back, and they took off into the sky.

Over the next couple weeks, Elmer and Peacock—whose real name was Samuel—taught themselves how to fly. They explored together, the three of them, Merrygold riding sometimes on Samuel, sometimes on Elmer.

They often flew over the ocean, where the whales spouted hello and goodbye.

But soon, Merrygold started to grow weak, from being out of the water for too long. She didn't want to leave Samuel and Elmer, though, and go back to the sea. So when they flew above a giant field of white flowers, Merrygold asked if they could land down there.

It was an ocean of daisies. Merrygold lay down in them, a great tiredness coming over her.

The two great beasts lay next to her, Samuel the peacock on her right, his feathers covering her bare chest, and Elmer the land dragon on her left, his wings supporting her head like a pillow.

And just like that, Merrygold fell asleep in the sun—a deep sleep, a sleep of peace and power.

Part 5:
San Francisco

Transitions #10: A Sleep
of Peace and Power

My Anna left this world three weeks ago. She was in a place of peace as she left us. Knowing we would be okay.

We. That's me and Phoenix, her son. My son now.

When Phoenix asks me questions, all I do is tell him the truth. It's all I know to do.

He asks me if she's coming back and I say no. I tell him we have her heart beating in ours forever, but that her body is gone.

That sweet, sweet body. Anna was made of gold, you guys. Glittering skin, hair as luscious as honey, and those red lips that smiled big and often. Someday I will post the photos I've taken of her here. One day, when I'm ready, I'll show you, and you'll see.

I want the whole world to celebrate her like I did. She was my superstar.

And when her hair went silver, you know she was even more interesting then. Like an elf, like some creature of the forest—oh, the wings on her as I imagined her flight from us. Even her death was charmed.

That was Anna. That was how she did everything, and it was how she died too.

She was so powerful. She was a visionary, in her own way.

When Phoenix asks me where she is now, I say I don't know. He says, "Maybe she's a fairy, living in the flowers. At night she glows like a firefly."

One thing is for sure: she's gonna be lighting our way for a long, long time.

Sammy, my love,

I never told you, but when you first called me "my love," my heart skipped a beat. I thought, I have been waiting my whole life for this person, and now she is here. Here to love me. I felt like the luckiest girl.

I still do, even as I write this from our room at the Plaza. Not even the looming end can take that away from me, because I had a love that was sweet and true. I had you.

I hope things are not too difficult with Phoenix. I know you are strong enough, though I'm sorry to put you through this. Parenting by fire. But you are a natural. I love how easy you are with him. I didn't know how to be like you. That's what I want him to learn—how to be easy and light in the world—and you are the perfect person to teach him.

I'm sorry I wasn't more supportive about your transness. I was too afraid, at first, to lose the woman I fell in love with. I just didn't understand; your blog helped me. And by the way, I love the blog. It's so you. Honest, and smart, and generous. I hope you can find and integrate all the parts of yourself in all the ways that feel right to you.

You guys will be back from your walk soon, and I ordered us room service. Thank you for going vegetarian with us, by the way. I don't think I ever thanked you for that. It means so much to me.

I love you and Phoenix so much it hurts. Sometimes I imagine the tumor is actually my love, so big it's eating me alive.

With a million kisses,

Anna

Dear Phoenix,

It's been a few days since I flew away, and I hope you are settling into your new home. I want you to know that I didn't want to leave you— I never would have chosen to leave you if I didn't have to. Okay?

You are the most magical, the most special, and I want all of your dreams to come true. Sam is going to help you.

At night when you lie down to sleep, I am holding you. I will rock you to sleep like I did when you were a baby. We had so much good time together, so many fun times, didn't we? Please never forget them.

Did you read this all by yourself? I am so proud of you. I hope you love your new school. Tell your teacher hi from me.

I miss you and love you with all my heart,

Mama

PHOENIX

I wanted to tell you, we live in San Francisco now. In case you ever want to come here. We live by Ocean Beach. Isn't that a funny name for a beach? It's so windy and there's always lots of dogs. Sam says maybe we can get one too. We go to the shelter every week to play with them. I read them books. I can read almost any word now.

I am typing this myself! Sam fixes my mistakes, so I guess she reads this too. Which is okay.

I was writing this to maybe have you read when I meet you, my dad. I always thought it would be fun to have a dad, but I guess now I do, kind of. Sam is like a dad and a mom. She says some days she feels more like a boy, and some days she feels more like a girl. I say "she" today, but tomorrow she might be a "he." It makes her seem magical.

Mama is gone. She drank a drink that made her die. I thought she would choke and cry but she just fell asleep. She was holding my hand, and then she wasn't. Her breath came out of her like air coming out of a balloon. I held her tight to try to keep the air in but it didn't work.

Mama wrote us a story, and every night Sam reads it to me. It's about a mermaid, and her friend the leafy sea dragon, and the peacock they meet. Really the mermaid is Mama, the sea dragon is me, and the peacock is Sam. Sometimes I dream about them, and even once I rode on the mermaid's back through the ocean, like they ride the dolphin in the story.

Sam says Mama named me Phoenix because I am strong, like fire.

I guess I probably won't meet you, now that she's gone.

I guess I should stop writing to you. I will always think of you when I eat mangos though, and imagine you up in a tree eating mangos all day, throwing down the pits to make more mango trees.

Me and Sam like to skate on the sidewalk above Ocean Beach, past the picture of Mama that Sam spray-painted on the wall. If we leave at the right time we can skate into the sunset.

So if you do ever come here, you can look for us there.

Fields full of gratitude for ...

Brittany Maynard
Dagmar Miura
Kimber Simpkins
Christopher Church
Katia Noyes
Nancy Millar
Peralta Elementary
Ocean Mandela Milan
Tammy Stoner